*"If I repaired c____
and we'd met, s____
in the produce aisle, would you go out
with me?"*

Jacqui's mouth twitched with what might have been a reluctant smile. "That's a lot of ifs."

Mitch shrugged, but didn't look away from her face.

"Okay, maybe," she said after a moment. "If all those things were true—which they aren't—I might consider going out with you. But even then, I doubt it would go anywhere. There are other things that would get in the way."

He figured they could work on those other things later. At least they had established that she wasn't entirely indifferent to him. He smiled. "Then let's pretend and see what happens. If it doesn't work out—then there's nothing lost, right?"

"I've never been very good at pretending."

He lifted her chin and brushed a light kiss over the lips he had been wanting to taste for much longer than he'd acknowledged even to himself.

Dear Reader,

I was once asked if I have a recurring theme in my writing. After thinking about the question for a while, I decided my theme is "home." By home, I don't mean a house or apartment—but a refuge. Home can be a physical place, certainly—where one feels safe and accepted and free to be oneself. Home can also mean family—biological relatives or friends to whom you are so close they feel like family. A soul mate, perhaps. A bond that soothes and sustains no matter where you are physically.

A Home for the M.D. explores this theme in more depth. Jacqui Handy has spent her entire life searching for a home; Dr. Mitch Baker has begun to take his own lifelong refuge for granted. They are drawn to each other, but before they can make that commitment, they must each define the meaning and importance of "home." Is it a place—or a feeling? Perhaps they'll each conclude, as I did many years ago, that the phrase "home is where the heart is" is the best definition of all.

Gina Wilkins

A HOME
FOR THE M.D.

GINA WILKINS

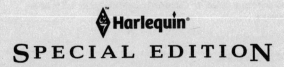

™ **Harlequin**®

SPECIAL EDITION

Recycling programs
for this product may
not exist in your area.

ISBN-13: 978-0-373-65605-9

A HOME FOR THE M.D.

Copyright © 2011 by Gina Wilkins

www.Harlequin.com

Printed in U.S.A.

GINA WILKINS

is a bestselling and award-winning author who has written more than seventy novels for Harlequin and Silhouette Books. She credits her successful career in romance to her long, happy marriage and her three "extraordinary" children.

A lifelong resident of central Arkansas, Ms. Wilkins sold her first book to Harlequin Books in 1987 and has been writing full-time since. She has appeared on the Waldenbooks, B. Dalton and *USA TODAY* bestseller lists. She is a three-time recipient of a Maggie Award for Excellence, sponsored by Georgia Romance Writers, and has won several awards from the reviewers of *RT Book Reviews*.

As always, for my family—John, Courtney, David, Kerry and Justin—my own definition of "home."

Chapter One

Dr. Mitchell Baker arrived at his rented duplex just as the firefighters extinguished the last flickers of flame. Glumly, he stood in the rain, surveying what remained of his home for the past six years, now a smoldering, blackened shell. Heavy clouds obscured what little natural light remained at 9:00 p.m., so the firefighters had set up portable lighting to assist them as they wrapped up their work. Normally, street lamps and security pole lights would glow at this hour, but the power was out on this whole street.

One of Arkansas's infamous summer storms had crashed through earlier, bringing high winds, booming thunder and dangerous lightning strikes. Somewhere on this tumultuous Thursday night in July, a tree had fallen over a power line, knocking out the electricity to this part of Little Rock almost two hours ago. Mitch's neighbor in the other half of the duplex—the woman he referred to as "the ditz next door"—had lit candles all through her rooms for light and then left to buy fast food for a late dinner. When she returned, the duplex was fully engulfed in flames.

Water trickled down his face and dripped off his chin. He reached up to swipe at his eyes with the back of one hand, clearing raindrops from his lashes. The rain was little more than a trickle now, but without a hat or raincoat, he was soaked. He made no effort to find shelter. Instead, he watched the firefighters gather their equipment and listened to the ditz next door as she told her tale to a woman who appeared to be a newspaper reporter. She wasn't even smart enough to make up an excuse for the fire, he thought with a shake of his wet head. She freely admitted that maybe the dozen or so candles she'd left burning had caught something on fire.

Maybe? He'd always believed the forty-something bottle-redhead was short a few watts in her mental chandelier, but now he figured most of the bulbs were permanently dimmed, to carry the metaphor further.

He thought regretfully of a few valued possessions he'd lost in that fire. A quilt his late grandmother had made that he'd used as a bedspread. Electronics equipment. Souvenir T-shirts from college and medical school activities and from his few travels. Pictures.

Fortunately, his laptop had been in his office at the hospital, and he kept files backed up online, so he hadn't lost the music and digital photos stored in his desktop computer. Most of his truly precious treasures—things that had belonged to his father and grandfather—were safely stowed in plastic bins in his mother's attic because the duplex had been too small to provide much storage. But still he regretted the things he'd lost. All his clothes, for example. The only clothing he owned now was a couple of shirts and two pairs of jeans stashed in his office and the sneakers he wore with the blue surgical scrubs in which he'd left the hospital.

"Dr. Baker? Are you all right?" The woman who lived in the nearest half of the matching duplex next door approached beneath a big, green-and-white golf umbrella. She and Mitch had met not long after he'd moved in, when he'd helped her retrieve her new kitten from a tree that stood between the two rental properties. That kitten was now a fat, lazy cat who liked to come visit him on Sunday mornings and beg for treats. Both Mitch and Snowball would miss those visits.

"I'm fine, Mrs. Gillis. Thank you."

She looked mournfully at the steaming remains of the house, then distastefully at the ditz, who was dramatically wringing her hands for the benefit of a television camera. "I figured that woman would cause a tragedy in this neighborhood, but I thought it would be because of her reckless driving. The way she zips down this street without any regard for anyone—and you know she hit Miss Pennybaker's mailbox just last week. Now this."

"At least no one was hurt, and none of the other houses were damaged." Mitch smiled reassuringly at her. "All the other stuff can be replaced."

"I'll miss having you as a neighbor. Not many nice young doctors want to live in this neighborhood. They all want to move out to those fancy houses in west Little Rock or some place like that."

When he'd moved into the rental, he'd been a very busy, twenty-five-year-old intern who'd been given a month's notice to find a new place after his former apartment had been sold to a developer. He'd looked for someplace available, convenient to the hospital and

reasonably priced, all of which he'd found in the tidy duplex in an aging but respectable midtown neighborhood.
He hadn't intended to stay more than a few months, but
those months had stretched into years while he'd spent
sixty to eighty hours a week at the hospital and what
little time was left over helping his widowed mother.

Now, two months into his pediatric orthopedic surgery practice, he could afford to buy or build, but he
couldn't think about that now. Not while almost all his
worldly possessions were still smoldering in front of
him.

Heaving a sigh, he rubbed a weary hand over his
face and urged his neighbor—his former neighbor, he
corrected himself—to get in out of the rain. There was
nothing anyone could do tonight. He assured her he had
a place to stay. He would crash at his mother's house
until he found someplace better.

A few minutes later, he climbed into his car and drove
away without looking back at the ruined duplex.

"Oh my gosh!"
Jacqui Handy was accustomed to fourteen-year-old
Alice Llewellyn's dramatic appearances, so she wasn't
overly concerned late Friday morning when Alice burst
into the kitchen with the exclamation. "What's wrong,
Alice?"

"My uncle Mitch's house burned down last night! To
the ground!"

Startled by the legitimate reason for her young
charge's agitation, Jacqui set down the copper water-
ing pot she'd been filling at the sink and turned quickly.
"Is he all right?"

"He's okay. He wasn't home. He was at the hospital."

Jacqui drew a relieved breath. She didn't know Mitch well, but she'd always liked him. She was glad he hadn't been hurt—but then, she'd have felt the same way about anyone, she assured herself.

"He lost everything, though," Alice added, her somber brown eyes a striking contrast to her mop of cheery light-brown curls.

"I'm very sorry to hear that. How did you find out about it?"

"I called Mimi to tell her about Waldo's new trick and she told me. Mitch spent the night with her last night."

Mitch's sister, Dr. Meagan Baker, had married Jacqui's employer, attorney Seth Llewellyn, three months ago. Seth had full custody of his teenage daughter. His ex-wife Colleen, Alice's mother, was a high-powered attorney at an international law firm based in Hong Kong. Seth had a distantly amicable relationship with his ex, who stayed in almost daily telephone contact with their daughter. Jacqui worked as full-time housekeeper and occasional cook and personal assistant for Seth and Meagan. In addition, she kept an eye on Alice and served as her daytime chauffeur when necessary. Alice considered herself too old to need a nanny, so they were all careful not to refer to Jacqui by that title.

"Mimi was pretty upset about the fire," Alice confided, pushing a hand absently through her tousled curls.

"I'm sure she was."

LaDonna Baker, widowed mother to Meagan, Mitch and Madison, was very close to her three offspring, all of whom had chosen to stay in Little Rock to practice medicine. She had embraced her new teenage stepgranddaughter into the family with affection and eagerness, and she and Alice had already grown very close.

Alice was the one who had given LaDonna the whimsical nickname of "Mimi," saying it fit in with the rest of the *M* names in the family. LaDonna had accepted the name with delight. Jacqui suspected having young Alice in her life had eased LaDonna's grief somewhat at the loss of her elderly mother at the end of last year.

"So, anyway," Alice continued, "Mimi's expecting company for the next week, so she doesn't really have a place for Mitch to stay until he finds a new place. And Madison has a one-bedroom apartment, so she doesn't have room for him, either. So I said why doesn't he stay here with us? We've got an extra guest room. I know Dad and Meagan would offer if they were here. So Mimi said that was a really good idea, if you and I don't mind, and she was going to call Meagan and tell her everything that happened and make sure it's okay."

"He's going to stay here?" Jacqui asked, following the rambling account with an effort. That was the part that stood out most to her.

She pictured Dr. Mitchell Baker, a tall, sandy-haired man with kind blue eyes and a warm smile that transformed his pleasantly homely face into full-out attractive. He was thirty-one, two years older than Jacqui. She had met him several times during the past fourteen months, although she could count on one hand the number of times she'd actually had a conversation with him. Those conversations had been brief and slightly awkward, at least on her part. For some reason she always became uncharacteristically tongue-tied around Mitch.

"I knew you wouldn't mind—you don't, do you?" Alice asked, suddenly aware, apparently, that she was making assumptions on Jacqui's behalf.

There seemed to be nothing gracious to say except, "Of course not."

Alice smiled with a flash of braces. "I knew you wouldn't."

Normally, Jacqui wouldn't be staying at the house herself. She had her own apartment across town. But Seth and Meagan had left only two days ago for a two-week trip to Europe on a belated honeymoon. They had asked Jacqui to stay with Alice, a request she had been happy to accept—and not just for the extra pay that would go into her savings for a down payment for her own house someday.

She told herself there was really no reason to be concerned about having a houseguest. She suspected that Mitch, a surgeon like his sister, would be at the hospital quite a bit. When he was here, Alice would keep him entertained. Jacqui would perform her usual role, staying quietly in the background. She was good at being a housekeeper, and she knew exactly how to play that part.

"Mimi's going to call you as soon as she talks to Meagan," Alice said on her way out of the kitchen. "I'm going upstairs to pack for the sleepover at Tiff's tonight."

Alice and her friends loved sleepover parties and were always looking for an excuse to have one. Because Tiffany was on the same swim team as Alice, they had decided to stay at Tiffany's house tonight and have her mother take them to a scheduled meet the next afternoon. Alice had assured Jacqui there was no need for her to attend this particular event, so Jacqui planned to use the time to catch up on some overdue chores including grocery shopping. She figured she might as well stay at her place tonight to dust and vacuum and grab a few extra things she needed here.

The phone rang only a few minutes later. She wasn't surprised that it was Meagan, calling to make sure there was no problem with her brother staying at the house for a few days.

"No problem at all," Jacqui assured her employer. "I'm glad to be able to help. Enjoy your vacation. Your brother will be fine."

"I'm so glad to know you're taking care of things there," Meagan said fervently. "I don't know what we would do without you, Jacqui."

Meagan's mother said much the same words when she called a few minutes later to discuss her son's plans with Jacqui. "He'll probably spend another night here with me and then come over there sometime tomorrow. You're sure you don't mind having an extra person in the house?"

"Not at all. I'll be cooking and doing laundry for Alice and me anyway. One extra houseguest will be no trouble at all. Neither Alice nor I will be here tonight, but I'll be back tomorrow morning, so he can come whenever he's ready."

"You're a jewel, Jacqui," LaDonna said warmly. "We're all so lucky to have found you."

During the past year or so, Jacqui had made a deliberate effort to make herself indispensable to the Llewellyn/ Baker family. She liked this job, and she wanted to keep it. In return, they had all been nothing but kind and generous to her. Maybe they even considered her an honorary member of the family.

She wasn't that presumptuous. Besides which, she had learned long ago that "family" was a word frequently used without real meaning. Family members—honorary or otherwise—were all too often expendable, in her experience.

Mitch's steps dragged as he climbed the steps to the front door of his sister's house Friday night. His mother had given him detailed instructions for letting himself in and disarming the alarm system. As tired as he was, he hoped he remembered her directives correctly. The last thing he needed tonight was to be arrested for breaking and entering.

It was after 11:00 p.m. He'd had a very long day of surgeries, meetings and a pretty-much mandatory appearance at a retirement party for one of the surgical department heads, followed by yet another couple hours of paperwork in his office. His amazing and efficient secretary had volunteered to spend her lunch hour picking up a few things for him so he hadn't had to wear scrubs to the party, which had been a casual affair fortunately. He now owned three pairs of khaki slacks, three white shirts, a comb and toothbrush, a few pairs of socks and a package of boxer shorts in addition to the two pairs of jeans, two polo shirts and electric razor he'd kept stashed at work. He'd had to wear sneakers to the party because Jean hadn't risked buying shoes for him.

It amazed him how kind and generous everyone had been at work. Other doctors, nurses, techs, office staff, everyone who'd heard word of the fire had offered condolences and any assistance he might need. His partners had volunteered to cover for him when he needed time to look for a new place and to replace his lost possessions, even though their schedules were all stretched to allow for summer vacations. A few people had even offered extra clothes and household goods. He'd been genuinely touched by everyone's thoughtfulness.

With a duffel bag holding his entire wardrobe clutched in his left hand, he used his right hand to quickly press buttons on the keypad located just inside the front door, resetting the alarm for the night. At least he had a place to sleep for a few weeks. He would have stayed with his mother, but his late father's two sisters had already planned to come for a weeklong visit. They were arriving tomorrow and even if his mom's house had been big enough to comfortably accommodate them all, he hadn't relished the idea of sharing a house even temporarily with the three women. His younger sister, Madison, was a third-year medical resident who lived in a one-bedroom efficiency apartment, so staying with her wasn't an option, either.

Moving in here seemed the ideal solution, and his sister and brother-in-law had agreed. In fact, they had interrupted their much-needed vacation to call and insist he make use of their spare room for as long as necessary.

He had planned to spend one more night at his mom's, but when he'd realized how late he was going to be, he'd called and told her he'd crash at Meagan's a night early instead. His mother had informed him no one else would be there tonight, so he didn't have to worry about disturbing anyone with his late arrival. Still, he made little noise as he climbed the stairs without bothering to turn on lights. Tiny, energy-efficient bulbs illuminated the steps for safety, providing a soft, cozy glow to guide him to the second story.

After the wedding in April, Seth and Alice had moved from their previous home across the street into

Meagan's house. Both houses in the upscale subdivision were approximately the same size, but this one had a pool in the roomy backyard—of primary importance to Alice. Seth had planned to put in a pool for Alice this summer, but they'd all decided it would be easier to simply settle in here. Seth's house was on the market now, although Mitch hadn't heard if it had sold yet.

Mitch hadn't actually visited this house often, even before his sister married Seth. He and his sisters usually gathered at their mother's place on the rare occasions when they were free to get together. He knew the master bedroom was downstairs and there were three bedrooms upstairs. Vaguely recalling that Alice's room was on the left of the staircase, he turned right, arbitrarily choosing the first door he encountered.

He was going to fall straight into bed, he thought with a yawn. He'd worry about unpacking his few belongings in the morning. Opening the door, he entered the darkened room.

He heard someone gasp loudly at the same time his foot made contact with something large and unyielding. Caught off guard, he fell forward, hands flailing in a futile attempt to steady himself, the duffel bag throwing him off balance. His shoulder made solid contact with the hardwood floor, knocking the breath out of him in a startled "oof!"

Lights blazed, assaulting his eyes. He squinted upward. What he saw made him flinch, just in time to keep from being beaned by a heavy, decorative brass candlestick.

"What the—? Jacqui, stop! It's me, Mitch. Meagan's brother!" he added in a rush, just to make his identity clear.

Her petite body still poised to strike or run, the

woman peered suspiciously down at him. Her short, near-black hair was tousled around her face. With her large, sleep-clouded dark eyes and softly pointed little chin, she looked even more elfin than usual—an adjective that had come to his mind the first time he'd met her a year or so earlier. He'd seen her only a handful of times since, but he'd recognized her instantly when she'd wielded the solid brass candlestick in a very efficient manner. He'd been damned lucky she hadn't bashed in his head.

She blinked her long, dark lashes a couple times as though to clear her vision, then stared down at him with a frown. "Dr. Baker?"

Shifting warily into a sitting position, he stretched his arm to make sure he'd done no damage to his shoulder other than the bruise he would undoubtedly sport tomorrow. "I'm sorry I scared you. I had no idea you were here. Mom said Alice had a sleepover, so you'd be staying at your own place tonight."

Jacqui tugged self-consciously at the mid-thigh-length hem of the New Orleans Saints jersey she wore for a nightshirt, revealing surprisingly long, slender legs for such a petite woman. "I was going to, but when I walked into my place earlier I found a leak that must have happened during the storm the other night. I guess some shingles were blown off or something. Anyway, the carpet was soaked, so I called the landlord, then gathered some things in my suitcase and came back here."

"Uh, yeah. I think I found your suitcase." He climbed to his feet. Now that he was upright, he stood a good nine inches taller than her barefoot five feet four inches. For such a little thing, she seemed more than capable of taking care of herself, he thought with a wry glance at the candlestick she still held.

Following his glance, she replaced the candlestick quickly on the nightstand. "Are you okay?"

"Yeah. Just bruised my pride a little. I'm really sorry I frightened you. I didn't know which bedroom to sleep in."

"I was under the impression you wouldn't be here until tomorrow."

"Last-minute change of plans. I hope you don't mind that I'll be staying for a few days."

"Of course not. It's your sister's house and she invited you. You have every right to be here."

She pulled at her jersey again, and he realized abruptly that she was probably uncomfortable with his presence in her bedroom. He reached for his duffel. "I'll move to the other guest room. It's across the hall, right?"

"Yes, directly across."

Moving toward the door, he spoke lightly. "Okay, then, I'll let you get back to sleep. Good night."

She remained standing in the center of the room. "Good night."

He stepped out in the hallway then couldn't resist glancing over his shoulder to say, "Oh, and Jacqui? You won't be needing that weapon again tonight."

Her mouth twitched in what might have been a reluctant smile as he closed the door firmly between them.

Turkey bacon sizzled in the pan while whole-wheat muffins browned in the oven. Sipping her first cup of coffee Saturday morning, Jacqui kept a close eye on the fluffy scrambled eggs cooking in the skillet in front of her. She'd heard Mitch showering upstairs, so she figured he'd be down soon. If he was like most of the men she knew, he'd be hungry.

On awakening this morning, and wincing when she saw her suitcase still lying on the floor, she had decided to put last night's awkwardness behind her. So Mitch had seen her in her nightshirt, with her hair all a mess and her cheek creased by her pillow. Big deal. Starting now, she was back in professional housekeeper mode. She wouldn't let that facade slip around him again.

"Good morning." Dressed in a new-looking white shirt and khakis, his sandy hair still damp from his shower, Mitch greeted her with a crooked smile that crinkled the corners of his clear blue eyes.

"Good morning, Dr. Baker." She removed the muffins from the oven with a potholder, setting the pan on a trivet. "I hope you like turkey bacon and scrambled eggs for breakfast. I wasn't sure if you'd have to report to the hospital this morning, so I thought I'd have breakfast ready just in case."

He studied the food with almost visible eagerness. "Looks delicious, but you didn't have to cook for me."

Having expected that comment, she shrugged lightly. "I was going to make some for myself anyway. Have a seat at the breakfast table. Do you drink coffee? Would you like orange juice to go with it? I have fresh-squeezed."

"You certainly don't have to wait on me. I'll get my own coffee." Moving to the coffeemaker, he poured a cup and carried it to the table.

Jacqui set a well-filled plate in front of him when he took his seat. "There's homemade jam and apple butter in those little crocks. Help yourself if you want some for your muffin."

Mitch picked up his fork, then raised his eyebrows when she didn't immediately join him at the table. "Aren't you eating?"

"I'm going to wash a load of cleaning cloths and then feed Waldo," she answered lightly. "Go ahead and eat. I'll have something when I've finished those things."

Mitch set down his fork. "I'll wait."

"Don't be silly, Dr. Baker. Your food will get cold."

"So will yours."

"I won't be long."

"Then it won't be a problem for me to wait, will it?" Leaning back in his chair, he picked up his coffee cup and took a sip, looking prepared to sit there all morning.

"Fine." Foiled in her plan to eat alone when he'd finished, she placed a spoonful of eggs and a muffin on a plate for herself and carried it to the table, setting it at the opposite end from Mitch. She retrieved her coffee mug from the counter, then took her seat.

Looking satisfied, he picked up a strip of bacon. "Just so we're straight—you work for my sister, not for me. I don't expect you to serve me or to wait until I've finished eating to have your own meal. Nor to address me as Dr. Baker. I answer to Mitch or Mitchell. I don't think my sister or her husband ask those things of you, either, for that matter. I've heard you call them Meagan and Seth, and I suspect you've shared a few meals with them."

"Well, yes," she admitted, stabbing her fork into her eggs to avoid looking at him. "But you're a guest."

"Hardly a stranger. We've known each other more than a year. And you're pretty much a member of my sister's family. There's no need for formality between us."

She spread a little jam on her muffin, busying herself with the task to avoid having to answer.

The table faced a sliding-glass door, on the other side of which lay a rock patio and beyond that, an inground pool. Mitch nodded toward the grinning yellow dog watching them through the glass, tail sweeping the air behind him. "Waldo didn't prove to be much of a watchdog last night. He never even barked when I parked outside and came into the house."

Following his glance toward Alice's beloved pet, Jacqui smiled. "As sweet as that dog is, I would never depend on him to guard the place. If he did catch someone sneaking in, he'd probably just bring up one of his toys and beg to play. I've always heard Labs are very territorial and protective, but Waldo...not so much."

"Maybe he'd react differently if someone were threatening a member of the family."

"I wouldn't be surprised if he showed some spirit then. Especially if it were Alice being threatened. Waldo does love Alice."

"Can't blame him. She's a great kid." He reached for his coffee. "Anyway, if Waldo were any kind of a guard dog, I wouldn't have taken you completely by surprise last night. Of course, that suitcase of yours did make a fairly effective warning system."

The corner of her mouth twitched at the memory of him sprawled at her feet, staring warily at the brass candlestick in her hand. It hadn't been funny at the time. She could still feel her heart pounding when she'd woken with the awareness that someone was in the room with her. But now she could see the wry humor in the situation. The way his eyes twinkled made her suspect he was struggling not to laugh.

Her humor evaporated when she remembered what had brought him there. "I'm sorry about your house. Alice and your mom told me it burned completely."

"To the ground. It was a rental, a duplex. My neighbor in the other half is a few fries short of a kid's meal. No one who's ever met her was surprised that she caused the fire."

She couldn't help being a little amused by the analogy despite the gravity of the situation. "She really left candles burning when she left the house?"

He shrugged. "That's what she said, and the fire marshal concurred it was the cause of the fire."

"Was it a furnished duplex?" Because she'd spent so much of her life moving from place to place, Jacqui hadn't collected many personal possessions. She always rented a fully furnished apartment. She looked forward to finally owning a home of her own that she could decorate with carefully chosen furnishings and maybe even a few nice pieces of art. Someday.

Mitch shook his head. "No, the furniture was all mine. Nothing too fancy. I'd lived there since my first year of residency and just gathered up what I needed to get by, but there were a few items I'll really miss."

"I'm sorry."

Although she could see the regret on his face, he downplayed his loss. "I had renter's insurance. I'd been considering moving to a somewhat larger place, anyway, now that I've finished my residency, but I didn't have to sign a lease there and I liked that. All I had to do was give a month's notice and I was free to leave at any time. Not many places let you do that."

"Not many rental places, no," she agreed, thinking of the one-year lease she'd recently renewed on her no-frills apartment. It was the first time ever that she'd stayed in one place long enough to actually renew a lease.

Recalling that Mitch had recently completed his surgical residency, she asked, "Will you buy a house now?"

He shrugged. "Haven't had time to think about it. I'm

not sure I want to commit to buying right now. I've considered working another year or so here in Little Rock and then maybe going somewhere else for a while."

"Really?" She recognized the restless look in his eyes all too well, having seen that same wanderlust in her father throughout her first seventeen years. Still, she was a little startled that one of the seemingly tightly knit Baker clan was considering a move away.

"Because of school and family obligations, I've never lived anywhere else," he admitted, scooping the last of his eggs onto his fork. "I'm not saying I will move, but it's nice to have options."

He'd leave. In her experience, once a man got an itch to roam, there wasn't much that would hold him in one place. As for herself, if she made the kind of money surgeons and lawyers made, she would buy a nice house with a tidy yard and settle down contentedly for the rest of her life. She'd had more than enough of drifting from place to place.

"Can I get you anything else?" she asked, nodding toward his nearly empty plate. "Another muffin? More coffee?"

He grinned, and she almost blinked in response to the brightness of that smile. Here was a man who never lacked for female companionship, she'd bet. He wasn't handsome, exactly, but definitely appealing. A single doctor with a killer smile—women probably lined up in hopes of catching his attention. She was surprised he was still single, but maybe he liked keeping his options open in that respect. Not that it was any of her business, of course.

"Didn't I just tell you I don't expect you to wait on me?" he asked teasingly.

She spread her hands and said matter-of-factly, "It's my job."

He studied her face a bit curiously but said merely, "Thanks, but I don't need anything else. I have some things to do at my office this morning. But breakfast was very good, thank you."

"I'll be doing some shopping later today. If you'll make a list before you leave, I can pick up any particular foods you like and whatever else you lack in the way of personal-care items. If you need anything—clothes, toiletries, whatever—I've picked up things like that for Seth when he was too busy to shop for himself."

His brow rose a little higher. "You really do make yourself useful, don't you? No wonder the family seems to think the house would collapse without you running it."

"I take pride in my work," she said a little stiffly, not entirely sure whether he was teasing or mocking her.

"That's the way I was raised, too. If you're going to do something, do it well."

It wasn't exactly the way she'd been raised—more a philosophy she'd adopted for herself—but there was no need to go into that. "There's a magnetic board on the side of the fridge. The Llewellyns usually leave a note there if they'll be home for dinner so I'll know to have something ready for them before I leave each evening. Sometimes they prefer to do their own cooking, but I usually cook two or three nights a week. You can write anything you need there and I'll take care of it."

Was she babbling? She did that sometimes when she felt uncomfortable.

Standing, Mitch carried his dishes to the sink, rinsed them and set them in the dishwasher without waiting for her to clear away after him. She could see this man was accustomed to taking care of himself.

"I'm not a picky eater, but I like to have fresh fruit on hand—any fruit, I like them all. I'll leave some cash for you to add to the tab. Neither you nor Meagan should have to pay for my food while I'm here. As for anything else, I'll have to make a mall run eventually and pick up some things—like shoes," he added with a wry glance at his sneakers. "I don't even know what else I need yet."

Despite her tendency to accumulate relatively few personal belongings, the thought of losing everything she owned was daunting. She was sure Mitch had lost things that were important to him in the fire. Sympathy made her speak a bit more warmly. "All right. But if you think of anything, just jot it on the list. Really, it's no trouble at all."

He gave her another one of those smiles that made her pulse trip a little. "That's very kind of you, Jacqui. Thanks."

Hiding her reaction to him behind a rather brusque tone, she turned away to rinse her own breakfast dishes. "You're welcome."

"I think we'll work out just fine as housemates," he said as he moved toward the doorway toward the stairs. "No reason at all to be concerned."

Housemates. Just the word made her mouth go dry. Which certainly seemed to her like a reason for concern.

Chapter Two

Later that morning, Jacqui finished making her grocery list. She had a generous household account to cover anything they needed, but Mitch had insisted on chipping in toward his food. She had intended to leave for the store more than an hour ago, but she kept getting delayed by things around the house that needed her attention— houseplants to water, furniture to dust, floors to vacuum, beds to change, laundry to do.

She knew every inch of this house like the back of her hand. It might belong to Seth and Meagan and young Alice, but she was the one who kept it running like a well-oiled machine, just as she had the house Seth and Alice had lived in previously. She was the one who'd done most of the packing, unpacking and arranging when the busy family had combined their households. They had decided which furnishings to keep and which to store, sell or give away, but Jacqui had supervised that process while the Llewellyns were tied up with their demanding schedules.

She had been greatly relieved that there'd never been any question of whether she would continue working for them after the wedding. With Meagan's hectic schedule as a general surgeon and attending physician in the teaching hospital, Jacqui's help was needed with the housework and with Alice.

They had established a routine that worked well for all of them. When the family was in town, Jacqui reported to work at around 9:00 a.m., after the senior Llewellyns had left for their jobs. During the school year, Alice had already been dropped off at school by that time; Jacqui picked her up every afternoon. Now that Alice was on summer break, the teen spent the days here at home or being chauffeured by Jacqui to various activities. Every day, Jacqui did the daily cleaning and laundry, ran family errands such as shopping and dry cleaning, then cooked dinner before leaving unless they'd notified her they had other plans for dinner.

Some people might have found her daily schedule boring, but she enjoyed it. She liked the family very much, and they paid her well for her services. Most of her weekends were free and she had time during her workdays to read and knit while doing laundry or waiting for the oven timer to buzz.

She was lucky to have found this family when she'd been looking for a full-time housekeeping job just more than a year ago. Her last employer had moved into a nursing facility and she'd needed a new position quickly. Only twenty-eight years old then, she hadn't been the typical housekeeper applicant. Her résumé listed many jobs in several states, only the latter two of which had been housekeeping positions. But the Llewellyns had taken a chance on her, and she was satisfied their gamble had paid off for all of them.

On the other side of the glass door, Waldo barked for attention, his feathery tail swishing rhythmically. He missed Alice today, she thought, stuffing the grocery list in her bag. He barked again, giving her his best please-notice-me grin. Caving, she set her bag aside. There was no hurry to go shopping; she might as well play with the dog for a little while to make him feel less lonely.

Waldo expressed his gratitude with full-body wiggles and eager swipes of his big, wet tongue. Laughing, Jacqui pushed him down. "You silly dog. You act like you haven't seen anyone in a month. I just gave you a good brushing this morning before I fed you breakfast. And Alice will be home in just a few hours. You're hardly neglected."

Panting, he leaned against her, gazing up with happy dark eyes. She sighed. "Okay, I'll throw your ball for you. But do not get me dirty. I don't want to have to change before I go shopping."

She didn't at all trust the grin he gave her in response to that admonition.

Half an hour later, she was still outside, tossing a tennis ball for the dog, who seemed to never run out of enthusiasm for the mindless game. He would have liked even more for her to throw the ball into the pool; there was nothing Waldo loved more than to throw himself into the water after a toy, especially on a hot July day like this one. But she left the gate to the pool firmly closed despite his blatant hinting. With a wet dog climbing all over her, there was no way she'd stay clean enough to go shopping.

"Okay, Waldo, last throw," she told him firmly,

raising the ball in preparation. Like his owners, she'd gotten into the habit of speaking to the big yellow Lab mix as though he could understand every word she said. And like them, there were times when she suspected he understood quite a bit. "One more time, and then I absolutely have to go do the shopping."

"Aw, just one more?"

Her heart gave a thump. She turned to find Mitch standing in the kitchen doorway, leaning against the doorjamb as if he'd been there a few minutes. "Don't encourage him," she said with a faint smile of greeting. "He'd keep me out here all day if he could."

"Can't blame him for that."

Giving the ball one last heave, Jacqui turned toward the house. Waldo collected the ball and then, sensing the game was over, moved resignedly to his water bowl. Jacqui followed Mitch into the kitchen and closed the door behind them.

She washed her hands thoroughly in the kitchen sink, saying over her shoulder, "You're back earlier than I expected."

"I try not to work full days on weekends, unless I'm on call. Usually have to go in for an hour or two, but more than that is just begging for burnout. Of course, there are plenty of times I get tied up there all day even then."

"I can imagine." She glanced at the microwave clock, noting it was just before noon. "Have you had lunch?"

"No. After that nice breakfast you made for us, I haven't been hungry yet."

"I'm just about to leave for groceries. I could heat a can of soup for you before I go, maybe make a sandwich, if you like."

"Have you had lunch?"

"Not yet. I'll probably get something while I'm out."

"Why don't I go with you? We can take my car. We can have a quick lunch and then I'll help you get the groceries."

She blinked. "You're offering to go grocery shopping with me?"

He laughed quizzically. "Why do you look so startled? How do you think I've gotten food for myself during the past decade that I've lived on my own? The grocery fairies don't visit this area, as far as I know."

"I just assumed a busy surgeon would pay someone to do that for him."

Chuckling, he shook his head. "Until a couple of months ago I've been a student or a resident. My extra cash has been going toward paying off student loans. I do my own cleaning, my own cooking—when I bother— and my own shopping."

"I'm sure you'd like to relax after working this morning. Just let me know anything you need, and I'd be happy to get it for you."

"If you'd rather I stay here…"

Something about his expression reminded her very much of Waldo's please-play-with-me face. She found herself just as unable to resist with Mitch. After all, she rationalized, he had lost his home. She supposed he was feeling at loose ends today, maybe in need of distraction, even if it was for fast food and grocery shopping.

"You're welcome to come along," she said lightly, tucking her bag beneath her arm. "That way you'll be sure to get exactly what you like."

He smiled. "Sounds good to me."

Her steps faltered a little toward the doorway, but she lifted her chin and kept moving. It was too late to back out now.

* * *

They had lunch at a bakery-café not far from the supermarket where Jacqui usually shopped. Mitch had a turkey panini with chips and a pickle spear; Jacqui ordered half a veggie sandwich and a cup of vegetarian black-bean soup.

Glancing at her plate, he cocked his head in curiosity. "Are you a vegetarian? I noticed you skipped the bacon at breakfast."

She shrugged lightly. "I'm not a true vegetarian. I like fish and chicken, occasionally, but I simply prefer veggies and fruits."

"I like veggies and fruits myself. If you prefer cooking vegetarian, that's perfectly fine with me."

"I have no problems cooking meat. Your brother-in-law is most definitely a carnivore."

Laughing, Mitch reached for his water glass. "Well, he is a lawyer."

She smiled wryly. "Low blow."

"Just kidding. I like the guy. I'm glad he and Alice are part of our family now."

"The three of them make a lovely family."

Jacqui had been a silent spectator during much of Seth's courtship of Meagan. Meagan had initially interviewed Jacqui for the job as Seth's housekeeper when his previous employee had fallen and broken her leg, but Meagan had been helping out only as Seth's friendly neighbor at the time. From the relative anonymity of her job, Jacqui had observed during the next few months while Seth and Meagan had grown closer, then moved apart. The busy attorney and harried surgeon had been afraid their demanding careers and other obligations would be insurmountable obstacles between them.

Jacqui suspected they had worried as much about hurting Alice as about having their own hearts broken. But love had overcome their fears, and they had become engaged at Christmas.

Jacqui had attended their small, tasteful wedding, and she didn't think she'd ever seen a happier couple. Since that time they'd managed to arrange their hectic schedules to allow as much time as possible for each other and for Alice. Jacqui liked to think her capable behind-the-scenes management of their household had smoothed the way for them, at least to some extent.

"Hey, Mitch."

In response to the greeting, both Mitch and Jacqui looked around. Three men in baggy shorts and T-shirts were passing the table on the way to the exit. All of them looked as though they knew Mitch, judging from the way they nodded to him.

"Hey, Nolan. Scott, Jackson. How's it going?"

"Been shooting some hoops in J-ville," one of the men answered for the group. "You playing football tomorrow?"

"Maybe. I'll have to buy some shorts."

"Heard about your house," another man spoke up. "Sorry, bro. Anything you need?"

Looking as though he appreciated the offer, Mitch shook his head. "I'm good, Jackson. Thanks."

"Let us know if you think of anything," the first guy said again, looking at his companions as if for confirmation. They all nodded earnestly.

"Thanks, Scott. Maybe I'll see you tomorrow."

"Co-ed game," Scott added with a flirtatious smile toward Jacqui. "Be sure to invite your friend."

Mitch nodded. "I'll do that."

"Friends," Mitch explained after the trio had moved on.

"Yeah, I got that."

"Hadn't even thought about losing all my sports gear yet." He toyed with the remains of his sandwich, regret etched on his face.

"I'm sorry. It must be difficult to lose everything."

"It's daunting," he agreed. "But I suppose it's a chance to start fresh, too. Too much stuff just ties you down, you know?"

She wouldn't know about that. She'd never really owned enough that she couldn't throw everything in her car and move on a moment's notice. But it wouldn't always be that way, she promised herself. As soon as she could afford her own place, she couldn't wait to buy furniture and decorations. Things that made a house a home.

"I guess clothes are my most immediate need," Mitch mused. "I'm supposed to go on a trip to Peru in September, so I'll need clothes and luggage for that."

"Peru?" she asked, hearing a hint of excitement in his voice. He seemed to want her to ask him to explain, so she figured she might as well humor him for the sake of conversation.

He nodded. "Some friends are making a five-day Machu Picchu trek. Eight days total for the trip. It's something I've always wanted to do."

"Then you should go."

"The fire came at a bad time—not that there's ever a good time for a fire—but now I've got to make living arrangements and replace some stuff. Still, I think I'll be able to put it all aside and take a week off for the trip. To be honest, it'll be my first time out of the country, other than a four-day senior trip to Cancun, Mexico, the summer after high school graduation. Been too busy studying and working to go anywhere since."

She wondered if that trip would assuage the restlessness she sensed in him—or merely whet his appetite for more traveling. From what she'd seen, when a man got it in his head that he wanted to travel, there wasn't much that could hold him back. "I hope you get to go and that you have a great time."

"Thanks. Have you been out of the country?"

"My dad decided to move us to Canada once. I must have been about nine. We stayed in Vancouver for about six months, then moved to Seattle for a while."

"So you didn't grow up in Arkansas."

"We moved a lot," she said somewhat evasively. "We lived in Arkansas for a year when I was in junior high, and it was always one of my favorite places, so when I had the chance, I came back here."

"Where else have you lived?"

He seemed to be making conversation rather than prying, but it still made her a little uncomfortable to talk about her past with this man whose life had been so very different. "I've lived for at least a brief time in fifteen states."

"Fifteen states? Wow. For someone as young as you are, that's a lot of moving around. Especially since you've been working for my sister's family for a year."

"A little over a year, actually. I worked for another man in Arkansas—in Hot Springs Village—for almost a year before that, so I've been back in this state for a while. As for my age, most people think I'm younger than I really am. I'm twenty-nine."

"Do your parents still move often?"

She nodded. "I can't imagine my father ever staying

in one place for long, and my mother seems content to follow him around the country."

The last she'd heard, they'd been in Arizona. But it had been a couple months since she'd talked with her mother, so they could very well have drifted someplace else since then. For the past dozen years, especially, they'd been unable to settle anywhere for long. During those twelve years, they had traveled on their own while Jacqui followed a different path.

"Do you have any siblings?"

The question still made a hard lump form in her chest, even after all this time. "I had a sister. She died."

Although she wasn't looking at him, she sensed Mitch searching her face. She wondered if he'd heard the guilt that always swamped her when she thought of Olivia.

"I'm sorry," he said quietly.

"Thanks." She reached for her purse. "If you're finished with your lunch, we really should get the groceries. I'm supposed to pick up Alice at four."

"I'm done." He swallowed one last gulp of his tea and then stood.

Jacqui moved toward the exit without looking back to see if he followed.

Mental note to self. Don't ask Jacqui personal questions.

Mitch glanced sideways at the woman in his passenger seat as he drove toward the supermarket she said she preferred. He couldn't help being curious about her, despite her reticence about her past. Or, just as likely, because of it.

Although he wouldn't have called her chatty, their conversation had been going pretty well during lunch until he'd started asking questions about her family.

He had definitely hit some raw nerves there. Her relationship with her parents was obviously strained, and her old pain from losing her sister had been almost palpable.

What had it been like for her, growing up without strong roots to either a place or her family? So strongly connected to his own mother and sisters, and to the memory of the father he had loved deeply, and never having lived anywhere but central Arkansas, Mitch couldn't really identify with her experiences, but he would have liked to hear about them. Not that her past was any of his business, of course. Although circumstances had brought them under the same roof for the next couple of weeks, they were merely acquaintances, nothing more. Maybe by the time he moved on, they could at least claim to be casual friends.

It was her suggestion that they stop at a sporting goods store they passed on the way to the supermarket. "If you're going to play football with your friends tomorrow, you'll need clothes," she said.

Stopped at a red light, he looked at the store, thinking how convenient it would be to save at least one extra shopping trip. "You're sure you don't mind?"

"Of course not." She motioned for him to turn into the shopping center in which the sporting goods store was located.

"I won't be long," he promised. "Just need a few things."

"No reason to rush. We have a couple of hours to shop before Alice gets home."

The casual assurance made him realize that her hurry to leave the lunch table had been more related to their conversation than her schedule for the remainder of the day. No surprise.

"Kind of warm for a football game, isn't it?" she asked, glancing at the blazing sun in the cloudless sky.

He shrugged as he pulled into a parking space and killed the engine. "We dress cool, drink plenty of water. We don't start until six, so even though it's still hot, the sun has gone down some. By the way, Scott was serious about you being welcome to join us, if you like. The games are co-ed, and we have several women who show up regularly to play."

"Since it's co-ed, I take it you play flag football? Not tackle?"

He realized only then that she was under a misconception about the invitation his friend had extended. "Wrong game."

She caught on before he had the chance to explain. "Not American football. Soccer."

"Yeah. Scott was being pretentious, I guess."

She shrugged and reached to open her door. "The rest of the world calls it that."

"But in this country, it's reasonable to assume he was talking about our football. Scott likes to catch people in that assumption and correct them with a worldly indulgence toward their naiveté."

"Sounds kind of jerky."

Amused by her blunt assessment, he nodded. "He can be. But he's okay, on the whole."

Jacqui didn't look mollified. "I don't like it when people try to make other people look stupid. Your sister and brother-in-law would never do that, and they're pretty much the smartest people I know."

He hoped she didn't think he'd been having fun at her expense. "No, they wouldn't. And I—"

But she was already out of the car, the door snapping shut behind her. Mitch sighed.

Forty-five minutes later, he tagged behind Jacqui as she wielded a shopping cart through the Saturday-crowded supermarket aisles. She selected her groceries with even more care than he'd used in grabbing supplies at the sporting goods store while she'd browsed the sneakers collection.

She seemed to have no trouble being friendly with other people. Apparently, she knew quite a few employees of the supermarket. Several of them greeted her with obvious recognition and Jacqui responded with friendly smiles.

"How's the new baby?" she asked a young woman arranging roses in the floral department.

"He's doing great," the woman replied, beaming. "You wouldn't believe how fast he's growing. He loves the little stuffed bear you knitted for him. It's so soft and cuddly, and he always smiles when I give it to him."

"I'm glad he's enjoying it."

The florist eyed Mitch surreptitiously as she asked Jacqui, "Need any flowers today? We got some pretty lilies in this morning."

"No, not today, thanks, Latricia. Maybe next time."

A portly man behind the deli counter grinned broadly when Jacqui approached a few minutes later. "Well, hello there, sunshine. The little missy isn't with you today?"

"She had other plans today, Gus." She glanced at Mitch. "Alice likes to come shopping with me sometimes."

"That little girl does love her cheese," Gus commented with a chuckle. "What can I get for you today?"

Mitch stood back and watched as Jacqui placed her order. He was struck by her attention to detail even with simple luncheon meats. She'd been the same way with the other groceries now stacked in the cart, reading ingredients, comparing prices, making each choice with a frown of concentration. He enjoyed watching her at work—and she was very much on the job.

If only she could relax with him as she did with the store employees. Surely she wasn't intimidated by him? He could think of no reason at all for that to be true.

Maybe she just didn't like him? His ego twinged at the possibility. Was he really so conceited that he assumed everyone should like him? He believed most people liked him well enough, with a few exceptions he didn't much like either. But maybe there was something about him that rubbed Jacqui the wrong way.

He'd just have to see if he could manage to rub her the right way.

That errant thought made him shift his weight uncomfortably. He studied her from the corner of his eye as she took a smiling leave of the man in the deli.

He would be on his best behavior for the next few days, he promised himself. Whatever he might have done to annoy her, he would do his best to change her mind. He wouldn't mind having Jacqui smile at him the way she smiled at her friends here in the supermarket.

If Alice hadn't gotten enough sleep the night before, it didn't show during dinner that night. She chattered nonstop to her uncle throughout the meal, continued to talk while she helped Jacqui clean up afterward, then babbled even more when they joined Mitch in the family room a few minutes later. Jacqui settled in a chair in the corner beneath a bright reading lamp and pulled out the knitting bag she always kept nearby while Mitch and Alice surfed the TV channels for something they both enjoyed.

Mitch glanced Jacqui's way during a momentary lull in Alice's monologue. "What are you working on?"

Figuring he was trying to be polite and include her in the conversation, she lifted her project to show the ruffle-edged black scarf she was halfway through. "It's a scarf."

"Nice. Is this for your friend's store? Meagan mentioned you sell your knitted stuff at a boutique," he added.

She nodded. "A friend in Santa Fe sells handmade accessories in her shop. I met her when I lived there a few years back and I've been sending her stuff ever since. Mostly scarves, although occasionally she asks for baby blankets or hats or fingerless gloves, which are popular right now."

"How long have you been knitting?"

"Since I was a kid." A friendly neighbor had taught her the basics when her family had settled briefly in a trailer park in Utah. The woman had tried to teach Olivia, too, but Olivia hadn't been interested. Jacqui, however, had loved the hobby, something portable she could take with her wherever they went. She had guarded the needles that sweet lady had given her as if they were made of gold and had hoarded the yarn she'd purchased with odd jobs money or the occasional allowance from her parents.

The hobby had long since paid for itself. She would never get rich selling her handcrafted wares in the boutique and on the internet, but she kept herself in yarn and needles and rarely purchased gifts when she could make them herself. She made her own sweaters, scarves, gloves and hats and even made shopping bags, dishcloths and socks.

She was delighted that Alice had been knitting for almost a year. Alice had begged Jacqui to teach her last summer and she'd gotten quite good at it since. Jacqui enjoyed sharing her knowledge, the way that nice neighbor had done with her all those years ago. Alice liked knitting soft little stuffed animals in pastel yarns, which she then donated to the local children's hospital. The same hospital where her uncle Mitch worked, Jacqui thought, glancing at the pediatric orthopedic surgeon on the couch.

"Everything on TV is boring, Uncle Mitch. You want to play a game?" Alice asked hopefully.

"Sure, that sounds like fun," he said, looking as if he meant it. "What have you got?"

She jumped up eagerly and retrieved a stack of games from a cabinet under a built-in bookcase, setting them on the well-used game table in one corner of the comfortable family room. Generally eschewing the video games most kids her age loved, Alice was instead a fiend for board games, nagging anyone available into playing with her. Jacqui was roped into games fairly often, especially with Alice out of school for the summer.

Alice and Mitch selected a game, sat at the table and then both looked expectantly toward Jacqui.

"Can I get you anything to drink during your game?" she asked, motioning with her knitting toward the doorway.

"Come play with us, Jacqui," Alice urged, patting an empty chair at the table.

"Oh, I—"

Alice gave her a pleading, puppy-dog-eyes look that

would have put Waldo to shame. "Please. Games are more fun with three."

"I wonder if I should resent that," Mitch mused aloud.

Both women ignored him. Conceding to Alice's expression, Jacqui set aside her project. "All right. But just for a little while."

Two hours later, they still sat around the game table. Empty soda cans sat beside Alice and Mitch, and Jacqui had just finished her second cup of hot tea. Crumbs were the only thing remaining on the plate of cookies Jacqui had brought out earlier. Scribbled score pads documented individual victories in the games they'd played that evening.

She was startled to realize how much time had passed when she glanced at the clock on the mantel. Those two hours had flown by in a blur of rolling dice and laughter. Mitch and Alice were cute together. A stranger observing them would never have believed they'd known each other only a little longer than a year, that Mitch had not known his niece-by-marriage all her life. He teased her and chatted with her with an ease that proclaimed family bonds. At least the type of family bonds Jacqui had observed while working in this household. Not so much in her own.

How might her life have been different, she wondered idly, if her own family had spent time around a table, laughing over a board game? Or even just chatting over dinner? How might she have been different?

A memory popped into her head, dimming her smile. She and Olivia sat cross-legged on the floor of a cheap motel room, playing Monopoly with a battered, salvaged set. They'd replaced the missing game tokens with different-colored pebbles and had made their own deeds and play money with scraps of paper. They'd had a few little plastic houses and hotels and enough instruction cards to make it possible for them to play. She'd been maybe twelve at the time, which would have made Olivia ten.

She remembered the wistfulness in Olivia's smile when she'd earned enough scrap-paper money to buy a house.

"Don't you wish it was real?" Olivia had asked, studying the little green plastic house in her hand. "Don't you wish we could really buy a house and live in it forever?"

"Not likely," Jacqui had answered with a brusqueness designed to hide her own old longings. "Dad would be ready to move on before we even mowed the grass the first time."

"I'd like to mow grass." Olivia set the little plastic house carefully into position on the game board. "When I grow up, I'm going to have a house with a big yard and I'll mow the grass and plant flowers. Maybe I'll have a garden and grow peaches. I love peaches."

"You don't grow peaches in a garden. You grow them in an orchard," Jacqui had corrected with the wisdom of her additional two years.

"Then I'll have an orchard," Olivia had replied, unperturbed.

Jacqui snapped back into the present when Alice demanded her attention.

"Let's play Monopoly now!" the teen suggested with an eager look at the stack of games they hadn't already played.

Because there were only a few games left in that stack, Jacqui found no particular significance in Alice's choice, despite the coincidence. Still, her throat clenched enough that she had to clear it silently before replying. "That's all for me tonight, Alice. It's getting late, and I have a few things to do before bedtime."

Alice sighed, but didn't argue, to Jacqui's relief. When Mitch announced that he had early hospital rounds to make the next morning, Alice accepted that game night was over and began to put away the supplies.

Mitch helped Jacqui clear away the remains of their snacks. Carrying empty soda cans to the recycling bin in the kitchen, he smiled down at her when they almost bumped into each other as he reached around her to drop the cans in the bin. "Sorry."

This usually roomy kitchen had never felt as small as it did at that moment, with Mitch standing right in front of her and the kitchen counter at her back. All she'd have to do was take one small step forward and she'd be in his arms, plastered against him. Not that she intended to do anything of the sort, of course. It was strictly an observation.

Mitch studied her face for a moment, making her wonder what he might see in the expression she tried to keep carefully blank. And then he moved back a few steps. She drew in air, realizing she'd held her breath while he stood so close. What was it about this man that flustered her so much?

He moved toward the doorway. "I'm going to do some paperwork in my room, then turn in. I need to be at the hospital by six in the morning for a breakfast meeting with a partner. Told my mom I'd have lunch with her and Madison and our aunts, then I'm heading to the mall to buy a few things. Tomorrow evening I'll be playing soccer with the guys, so I won't be around here much."

She nodded, telling herself she should be relieved he wouldn't be underfoot the next day.

"Good night, Jacqui."

"Good night." He didn't seem to like it when she called him Dr. Baker, but she wasn't quite comfortable using his name yet, so she tended to avoid calling him anything.

He didn't look back when he left the room. She knew that because she watched him until he was out of her sight.

Two more weeks, max, under the same roof. She could do this. She assumed the novelty of him would wear off after a couple days of proximity. At least she hoped it would. She wasn't sure how much she could take of having her pulse race this way every time Mitch stood close to her.

As he climbed into the guest bed that night, Mitch wondered what it was about a suggestion of playing Monopoly that had made Jacqui's dark eyes go so bleak it had made his heart hurt for her. The most obvious explanation was that it had something to do with her late sister. Childhood memories, perhaps?

She hadn't said how long her sister had been gone, but it was apparent that the loss was still raw. He imagined what it would be like to lose one of his own sisters, and the pain was so immediate and so piercing that he put the thought quickly out of his mind. He didn't even want to consider the possibility. Losing his possessions was a minor inconvenience; losing members of his family— well, that was very hard for him to handle. He'd already lost one parent, his beloved dad, and that had been a horrible time for his whole family. It had been difficult enough saying goodbye to his grandmother last year, and they had all been braced for months for her death.

He didn't like seeing pain in anyone's eyes, but for

some reason it had especially bothered him to see Jacqui looking so unhappy, even momentarily. That sadness had been in such stark contrast with her laughter only moments before whatever memory had assaulted her.

She'd seemed to have fun during their game session with Alice. She'd teased along with him and his niece, and he'd been struck by her soft, rich laughter. For those two hours, she had even lost some of the reserve she usually showed around him—and that he still couldn't understand. He'd found himself having to make an effort to concentrate on the games rather than the glint of pleasure in her pretty, dark eyes.

Lying on his back in the darkened room, he stared upward, seeing Jacqui's face rather than the shadowed ceiling. Despite her obvious and bewildering wariness of him, he still found himself drawn to her.

He'd been intrigued by her from the first time he'd met her. He'd been surprised that the housekeeper his sister and her new family had raved so much about had been a rather gamine young woman rather than the stereotypically sturdy matron he'd vaguely envisioned. He'd admired her big, dark eyes, pointed little chin and soft, nicely shaped mouth, and although he usually was attracted to long, wavy hair, he'd liked her tousled pixie cut. It suited her.

As busy as he'd been the past year, and as awkward as it would have been to pursue his sister's employee, he'd done nothing about his initial tug of attraction to Jacqui. But now that they were under the same roof and spending more time together, the fascination was only growing harder to ignore. He was still busy, and it was still awkward—not to mention that she'd given him no encouragement at all—but maybe they could at least be friends by the time he moved into a new place. Maybe in the future she would smile warmly when she saw him, rather than that politely distanced expression she usually wore when he was around.

He'd like that.

Chapter Three

Jacqui had no intention of attending Mitch's soccer game. She knew very little about soccer, and she still winced at the way she'd reacted to Mitch's pretentious friend's affectations. She doubted she'd have much in common with a bunch of highly educated soccer enthusiasts—or football, as Scott had referred to it. To her, football would always involve pads and helmets and "Hail Mary" passes and touchdowns, but whatever.

She hadn't counted on Alice wanting very much to go.

"Mitch said there are usually some other kids my age hanging around to watch," Alice explained. "They don't let anyone younger than sixteen play because they're afraid the kids might get hurt playing with adults, but sometimes there's a kids' game on the next field. And sometimes they need help with carrying water and chasing soccer balls and stuff like that. Besides, I want to watch Mitch play. I bet he's really good."

"It's going to be pretty hot at the park today," Jacqui warned. "In the mid-nineties, according to the weather forecast."

Alice shrugged. "It's always hot in July," she said pragmatically. "Can we go, please?"

"Well, um—"

"You could just drop me off if you don't want to stay. Mitch can bring me home."

Jacqui envisioned Alice wandering around the crowded park alone while her uncle was engrossed in his game. Although Alice was fourteen and fairly level-headed for her age, Jacqui didn't like the thought of her being entirely on her own in such a public place. And what if Mitch wanted to go out for beers or something with his friends after the game?

"I thought maybe you and I could go to a movie this afternoon," she suggested in a weak bait-and-switch attempt.

Alice wasn't falling for it. She shook her head. "There's nothing I really want to see right now. I'd rather watch Mitch's soccer game."

Jacqui sighed heavily. "Fine. I'll take you."

Had she conceded too easily? Was her capitulation entirely a result of not wanting to disappoint Alice? Was it possible she secretly wanted to see Mitch at play, herself?

Frowning, she pushed a hand impatiently through her hair. "We don't have to stay for the whole game if it gets too hot or if you get bored."

"Okay." But Alice was grinning broadly in anticipation, seemingly undaunted by the risks of heat or boredom. Jacqui resigned herself to a long stay at the soccer field.

"Can we take Waldo? I'd keep him on the leash."

"No." Jacqui had no intention of backing down on that issue, even if Alice begged. Waldo was a sweet dog, but he was rambunctious when he got excited. Alice walked him around the neighborhood on his leash nearly every day and Jacqui drove them occasionally to the nearest dog park, but any new environment sent him into a frenzy of hyperactive exploration despite his obedience training. Because Alice wanted to watch the game, that meant Jacqui would be stuck at the end of Waldo's leash. "Not this time."

Alice seemed to consider arguing for a moment, then she must have decided to quit while she was ahead. "Okay, maybe next time. I'm going up to decide what to wear."

Studying Alice's pink-and-white-striped T-shirt and denim shorts, Jacqui asked, "What's wrong with what you're wearing?"

Alice rolled her eyes. "I just said there could be kids my age there."

That was supposed to be an explanation? Jacqui shook her head in bemusement as Alice dashed toward the stairs. She glanced down at the ultra-casual oversize T-shirt and leggings she'd worn for the light housework she'd done that morning. She supposed it wouldn't hurt to change. Not because she cared about trying to impress anyone, but because this rather heavy fabric could be uncomfortable in the heat. And if she chose an outfit that was a bit more figure-flattering—well, one should always try to look one's best when in public, right?

When they left the house half an hour later Jacqui wore a sleeveless yellow shirt of thin, cool cotton paired with khaki capris and leather flip-flops. She was still casual, but the soft yellow looked good with her dark hair and eyes, she decided.

After consulting with Jacqui on at least three different outfits, Alice had settled finally on a screen-printed, scoop-neck, purple T-shirt and a different pair of denim shorts. Glittery purple flip-flops revealed her purple-painted toenails. She'd tied her curly hair into a sassy ponytail and wore as much makeup as her father allowed—a touch of mascara and tinted lip gloss. The result was fresh and cute and much too casual to suggest she'd agonized for a good twenty minutes over the choices.

The spreading North Little Rock park was still crowded at six on this Sunday evening. Plenty of people had taken advantage of the slight cooling of the day to make use of the 1,600-acre park's picnic areas, hiking, biking and equestrian trails, golf course, tennis and racquetball courts, fishing lake, and sports fields for baseball and soccer and disc and miniature golf. Playgrounds and a small amusement park drew families with younger children. Jacqui had brought Alice to a birthday party at one of the pavilions there last spring, and she'd spent a couple hours exploring the park while Alice enjoyed the party.

Following the directions Mitch had left for them, they found the soccer field easily enough. But it wasn't until Alice spotted Mitch that they were sure they'd found the right group because so many other games were going on around them.

Grinning, he loped toward them. "Glad you could make it. We're just about to start. You want to play, Jacqui? The teams aren't really that formal. Anyone who wants to join in is welcome."

She had hoped the passing hours had given her time to brace herself for seeing him again. She'd told herself that increased exposure would somewhat soften the jolt of attraction that always hit her at the sight of him. No such luck. His sandy hair was tousled, his lean body nicely displayed in a blue soccer shirt and black shorts, his engaging smile warm and contagious. The too-familiar jolt hit her so hard she almost took a step back in response as she struggled to remember what he'd asked. "Um, no, thank you. I'll just watch with Alice."

"You're sure? We have a lot of fun."

She motioned toward her flip-flops. "Wrong shoes. Besides, I don't know the game that well."

Someone called his name from across the field. Or pitch, as Alice had referred to it. Mitch glanced that way and gave a brief wave, then looked back at Jacqui and Alice. "I'd better get back to the team."

"Good luck with your game," Jacqui encouraged.

"Thanks." He turned and dashed toward his friends. They weren't wearing uniforms, exactly, but Jacqui noted that most of the players on Mitch's side of the field wore blue shirts.

She couldn't resist one admiring look at Mitch's firm backside before she made herself turn to Alice. They'd brought folding canvas chairs stowed in shoulder-strap bags, and Jacqui carried an insulated tote bag in which she'd packed bottles of water and a few healthy snacks in case Alice got hungry. Mitch had told Alice the match would last almost two hours counting breaks. If Alice wanted to stay for the entire game, they would be eating dinner later than usual.

In addition to the chair bag slung over her shoulder and the insulated tote, Jacqui carried a patchwork crafts bag that held her latest knitting project. She couldn't sit that long without keeping her hands busy. Her knitting was so automatic by now that she would have no problem watching the game and finishing the scarf at the same time.

There weren't a lot of spectators for the casual game. Most of the people in attendance were participants, either on the pitch or lined up on the sidelines waiting for someone to get winded and need a rest. Each team seemed to have an unofficial coach who kept their side organized, and a couple of volunteers served as officials, running up and down the field and enthusiastically blowing whistles. A great deal of noise and laughter accompanied the good-natured rivalry.

"It's doctors versus lawyers," Alice confided with a laugh, nodding toward the competitors while she and Jacqui set up their chairs on a patch of grass where they could see the action. "The lawyers usually wear red shirts. Mitch said some people on both teams are students and some are older. He called himself one of the 'old guys.' I told him that was silly. He's not old. Not *really* old anyway," she added.

Jacqui couldn't help but smile as she took her seat. To a fourteen-year-old, thirty-one must seem fairly ancient, but at least Alice had conceded that Mitch wasn't quite ready for a cane and a rocking chair.

The match began with a flurry of kicks and head shots. The few spectators—most of whom seemed to be women with small children to entertain, keeping them from participating in the game themselves—cheered and called out encouragement. Although Jacqui made a determined effort to watch all the players, her gaze kept drifting to one in particular. Alice, too, watched intently for a short while, explaining rules of the game that Jacqui hadn't known, but then her attention wandered to a group of teenagers playing idly with a flying disc nearby.

"I think I know one of those girls from swim matches," she said. "Okay if I go talk to them, Jacqui?"

"Of course." Not particularly surprised that Alice's attention had drifted so quickly from the game she'd begged to attend, Jacqui almost advised the girl not to wander off too far, but she resisted the impulse. She had to keep reminding herself that Alice was growing up and understandably disliked being treated like a child.

As her knitting needles clicked in a soothing rhythm, she thought back to when she'd been fourteen. Much less sheltered and supervised than Alice, she'd been more worldly and mature at that age. Her parents had left their daughters alone for hours, sometimes for a couple of days at a time while they'd pursued their own ever-changing interests or worked odd jobs to keep the family in gasoline, cheap motel rooms and food—in that order. Jacqui had been responsible for getting Olivia and herself ready for school. Neither high school graduates themselves, their parents hadn't helped them with their homework or attended school programs with them. They hadn't set curfews or bedtimes, and they'd shown only occasional interest in their daughters' friends and activities.

Eddie and Cindy Handy hadn't been abusive parents. Just ineffective ones. They'd loved each other and their daughters, in their odd ways, but their own issues had prevented them from providing the sort of guidance and support their children had craved. They had grieved when Olivia died, so deeply that the gaping wound had been the final separation between them and Jacqui. They hadn't argued long when she'd told them at seventeen that she wanted to make her own path from that point. They'd stayed in touch in a desultory fashion—but they hadn't been a real family since. If, indeed, they had ever been.

She drew her thoughts abruptly to the present, wondering what had triggered that melancholy little trip into the past. The fact that she was surrounded by seemingly happy families in the park? That she was watching a group of doctors playing with a group of lawyers, making her wonder if any of them could imagine an upbringing like hers? She wasn't naive enough to assume that all these disparate professionals came from privileged or idealized backgrounds, but they had attained higher education, which made them different enough from her.

She turned her attention back to her knitting, telling herself she was being silly. She belonged in this park as much as anyone. And she was perfectly happy with the life she had chosen—despite her occasional vague longings for something she couldn't even define.

After forty-five minutes of play, the teams called a break for halftime. Alice drew herself away from her friends for a few minutes when she saw Mitch walking toward Jacqui.

"You're playing great, Mitch!" she said cheerily, bounding up to join them.

Jacqui smiled wryly, wondering if Mitch was aware of how little notice Alice had actually given to the game.

After taking a swig of a sports drink, he wiped his brow with a hand towel he'd brought in his sports bag and winked at Jacqui before answering his niece. "I'm glad you've been entertained."

Jacqui told herself the wink had only been conspiratorial, acknowledging Mitch's awareness of Alice's divided attentions. He hadn't actually been flirting or anything, so there had been no reason for her heart to skip a beat in reaction.

Mitch glanced at the knitting in Jacqui's lap. "If y'all are ready to go, don't feel like you have to stay until the end of the game for my sake."

"I'm not ready to leave yet," Alice said quickly. "I've been hanging out with some kids my age over at the picnic tables."

Widening his eyes in mock surprise, Mitch said, "I thought you'd been watching my game."

"I can see it from over there," she assured him. "Some of it anyway."

He laughed and tugged at the end of her curly pony-tail. "Just teasing. But what about Jacqui? Maybe she's bored sitting here by herself while you're hanging out with friends and I'm playing."

"Not at all," Jacqui answered candidly. "I'm enjoy-ing it. And I've made good progress on finishing this scarf."

"See?" Alice beamed approvingly at Jacqui. "There's no need for us to leave yet."

A whistle blew from the field, signaling that the game was about to start again. Mitch turned that direction. "Okay, see you both later then."

He jogged off without looking back.

"You really don't mind if I'm over there with the other kids?" Alice asked hesitantly before abandoning Jacqui again.

"I really don't mind," Jacqui assured her with a smile. "Have a good time."

"Thanks." Alice turned and hurried back toward the picnic tables, ponytail bobbing behind her. Jacqui picked up her needles again, her gaze on the field as the players assembled for the second half of the match. She'd lost count of the score, but she thought the doctors were ahead by one goal.

"I don't remember seeing you here before."

Her hands going still, Jacqui rested the almost-finished black scarf in her lap and turned to the woman who had greeted her from a nearby lawn chair. The woman must have set up there during the halftime break because Jacqui hadn't noticed her before.

"That's because this is my first time here," she replied with a faint smile.

"Watching a friend play?"

Jacqui laughed ruefully. "Actually, I brought a young friend to watch her uncle play, but she seems to have lost interest."

She intended to make it clear from the start that there was nothing between her and Mitch, even though she was attending his game. She doubted he would appreciate gossip or speculation about them among his friends and professional acquaintances, especially if it became known that she was his sister's housekeeper.

The other woman who was somewhere around Jacqui's age looked tall and curvy even sitting down. Her undoubtedly expensive white blouse and capris were crisp and spotless even in the heat. Her softly curled black hair framed a square face with perfect, milk-chocolate skin and wide-set black eyes, and her smile was friendly enough, if a little reserved. "I'm Keira. I'm here with my fiancé. Nolan."

Keira motioned vaguely toward a man on the field who looked familiar to Jacqui. Had he been one of the three who'd interrupted her and Mitch at lunch yesterday? She thought one of them might have been named Nolan.

"I'm Jacqui. It's nice to meet you."

Scanning the field, Keira asked, "Is Mitch Baker your young friend's uncle?"

She must have seen them talking a few minutes earlier. "Yes, he is."

"He's one of Nolan's pals. They get together all the time to play basketball or soccer or video games or poker. When Nolan's not at the hospital, he's hanging out with the guys. Rather than fight him about it, I just tag along whenever I'm invited. He's tried to talk me into playing soccer with them, but to be honest, I hate the game. All that running and sweating—not my style."

Jacqui chuckled in response to the frank admission. "Nolan's a doctor, too, I take it?"

"Anesthesiologist. He and Mitch were in the same medical school class."

Feeling a little wilted in the heat of the afternoon, Jacqui drew her half-finished bottled water from her tote. "I have an extra bottle if you'd like one," she offered.

"Thanks, but I have one. Have you known Mitch long?"

Keira appeared more bored than nosey. She didn't seem particularly interested in talking to any of the busy mothers swapping mommy stories nearby while keeping one eye on their kids and the other on the game. Maybe Keira thought she'd have more in common with Jacqui.

Doubting that, Jacqui answered candidly, "I've known Mitch about a year. I work for his sister's family."

The other woman looked toward the cluster of teens in which Alice stood chattering and giggling. "Are you a nanny?"

"Alice is a little old for a nanny, though I do keep an eye on her. I'm the housekeeper."

Keira blinked. "Oh. You don't—um…"

You don't look like a housekeeper. Jacqui finished the statement in her head, wondering how many times she'd heard it said in the past two years or so. Why did everyone think all housekeepers looked like Alice from *The Brady Bunch?*

She shrugged. "I enjoy my work."

After a moment, Keira said, "I'm a respiratory therapist. That's how I met Nolan."

"Sounds interesting."

"Most days," Keira agreed, still looking distracted by Jacqui's occupation.

A flurry of activity on the field captured their attention, and they watched as Mitch passed the ball to Nolan, who gave it a swift kick that sent the ball flying past the other team's goalie and into the net. Cheering broke out among Mitch's team and their few supporters on the sidelines. Jacqui clapped to demonstrate her own approval while Keira called out, "Way to go, baby!"

Preening for his fiancée, Nolan flexed victoriously until his teammates shoved him back into action for the next play.

For the next few minutes, Jacqui divided her attention between the game and her knitting while the other woman focused intently on the field, no longer in the mood for conversation apparently. She was almost surprised when Keira spoke again after a rather lengthy silence between them. "That girl you're with? Alice?"

Jacqui glanced instinctively toward her charge, frowning when she noted that Alice and a couple of other girls of about her age were gathered around a young man who looked to be three or four years their senior. The way Alice posed and giggled, it was obvious some serious flirting was going on. The other girls were performing too, all seemingly competing for the older boy's approval. He lounged against a tree, visibly basking in the attention, though he was doing his best to look "cool."

Jacqui told herself not to be concerned; it was normal for fourteen-year-old girls to practice their flirting skills, though she had never been much of a flirt, herself. She'd had too many other things on her mind at that age—like making sure she and her sister had school supplies and their homework turned in on time.

"What about Alice?"

"That boy she and the others are talking to is Scott Lemon's kid brother, Milo. He's eighteen or very close to it. How old is Alice?"

"Fourteen."

Keira nodded. "That's about what I guessed. Just giving you a heads-up."

"I appreciate it. Is it only the age difference that concerns you, or is there something more about him I should know?"

The other woman's hesitation was somewhat of an answer in itself. "I don't really know him well. I've just seen him hanging around a few times with Nolan and Scott and the other guys. He's Scott's half brother, I think—something like twelve years younger than Scott."

And Keira hadn't been impressed with what she'd seen—or heard—about the kid, Jacqui deduced. "Thank you. I'll keep a close eye on her."

"Good idea."

Alice ran back over to Jacqui's chairs only a few minutes later. Her eyes were alight with excitement, her cheeks unusually pink. "Okay if I go play miniature golf? I can get a ride home when I'm done."

Jacqui frowned. "You know that's not nearly enough information, Alice. Who would you be playing with and who would be driving you home?"

"Just some of the kids," Alice answered vaguely. "And Milo would bring me home. He's almost eighteen, and he has a driver's license and a car."

"Sorry. No."

"It's okay, Jacqui. His brother is one of Uncle Mitch's best friends. So it's not like he's a stranger."

Behind Alice's back, Keira looked studiously at the action on the field, pretending not to pay attention. Yet Jacqui saw the other woman shake her head slightly in response to Alice's argument, as if offering silent advice. Advice Jacqui hadn't actually needed.

"No, Alice. You aren't riding with a boy that neither your parents nor I have met."

"But Jacqui—"

"If you really want to play miniature golf with your friends, I'll come along. I can wait until you finish your game, then drive you home."

Alice wasn't satisfied with what Jacqui considered to be a rather magnanimous offer. "They'll all think I need a babysitter. What if Uncle Mitch says it's okay? I mean, Milo is his friend's brother, so Mitch would probably agree."

Jacqui glanced across the park to where Milo lounged against a tree, watching Alice with a look Jacqui didn't care for at all. "Your father left me in charge of you, not your uncle. And my answer is no. Either I accompany you to the miniature golf course and drive you home afterward, or you can stay here with me until the end of the soccer game. Or we can leave now—your choice."

There must have been a note of steel in her voice that Alice had never heard before. Alice blinked a few times, seemed to realize it would do her no good to argue further, then poked out her lower lip in a near-pout. "Fine. I'll just tell my new friends I can't go with them."

"It's your choice," Jacqui replied evenly. "You can make me the bad guy if you want, or you can tell them we have other plans if you want to save face."

Her expression supremely martyred, Alice turned on one heel and walked away, her posture expressing her dissatisfaction. Jacqui let out a low breath. In the just more than a year that she'd been charged with the responsibility of looking after Alice when her dad wasn't around, this was the first time the girl had even come close to a rebellion against Jacqui's authority. Alice had always been cheery, well-behaved, cooperative, eager—in other words, almost the perfect young teen in Jacqui's opinion. Sure, there had been some minor disagreements in the past year but not quite to this extent. And not with such high stakes, as far as Jacqui was concerned.

She had no intention of allowing Alice to get involved with a boy—much less an eighteen-year-old boy—while her parents were out of town. If it were up to Jacqui, it would be a couple of years yet before Alice was allowed to ride in cars with teenagers behind the wheel. Knowing Seth, she suspected he would agree with her on that point. If he'd had the same grim experiences as Jacqui, he would probably never let his daughter in the car with another teen, she thought darkly.

The soccer game must have ended during the confrontation. When she glanced at the field, the players were milling among each other, shaking hands and chatting amicably. Jacqui had no idea who'd won. She recapped her water bottle and slid it into the insulated tote, then folded her knitting and tucked it into its bag.

A towel draped around his neck, his hair and new clothes damp with sweat, Mitch walked toward her a few minutes later. He nodded toward Keira, who was gathering her things in preparation to join her fiancé, then smiled at Jacqui.

"Did you see me make that last goal? The winning one?"

Because he sounded so much like a kid hoping for a pat of approval, Jacqui hated to have to shake her head. "I'm sorry, I missed it. I guess I was talking to Alice. But congratulations."

Was there just a touch of disappointment in his voice when he responded? "Thanks. Where is Alice anyway?"

Jacqui waved a hand in the girl's direction. Following the gesture, Mitch looked that way, then frowned. "Is that Milo Lemon she's talking to?"

"So I was told."

"Yeah, not going to happen." He placed two fingers in his mouth and blew out a shrill whistle that carried over the noise of the slowly dispersing crowd. When Alice looked his way, he motioned for her to join them.

Even from where she stood, Jacqui saw Alice's reaction, but then the girl said something to Milo and the other girls and headed in their direction.

"Huh. I think I just got a teenage roll of the eyes," Mitch commented dryly.

"I know you did," Jacqui said, her own tone wryly empathetic.

"Think Uncle Mitch's whistle embarrassed her?"

"Oh, I wouldn't worry about it too much. She's just

in a teen mood today apparently. I've been the recipient of some of the attitude myself."

"And here I was hoping that sweet little Alice would just skip that moody, hormonal teen stage and go straight into responsible adulthood."

Jacqui laughed shortly. "Hold on to that dream, pal."

Both of them pasted on quick smiles when Alice joined them.

"We won, kid. By one goal. Scored by your uncle, I might add," Mitch boasted.

"Really? That's cool. Sorry I didn't see it. I was talking to some other kids."

"Good thing I have a healthy ego," Mitch murmured, looking only slightly deflated that neither of them had seen him make the goal.

"I was going to go play miniature golf with some new friends, but Jacqui said no."

Jacqui cocked an eyebrow. "I said I'd be happy to accompany you and drive you home afterward. The only thing I said no to was riding home with a teenage boy."

"You know Milo, Uncle Mitch," Alice said in an ingratiating tone. "His brother is one of your best friends."

"His brother is a friend," Mitch agreed. "I wouldn't say one of my best, but that's just semantics. And by the way, I agree a hundred percent with Jacqui. I wouldn't let you go riding around with Milo, either. Sounds like Jacqui made a nice offer to sit around here for another hour or so while you play mini-golf, by the way. She would probably rather go home."

Something in her uncle's tone made Alice stand a little straighter and carefully erase some of the discontent from her expression. "Thanks for offering, Jacqui, but I guess I'd rather go home, too," she said a bit hastily. "I need to take Waldo for a walk anyway."

Mitch nodded slightly in approval. "So I'll see you ladies in a little while."

"Will you be eating out, or are you joining us for dinner?" Jacqui asked him, using what she thought of as her "housekeeper voice" so he wouldn't think she was being nosey.

Wiping his face on a corner of the towel, Mitch replied, "If you're cooking, I'll join you. But don't go to any special trouble for me."

"Alice and I have to eat. I'll have something ready shortly after I get there."

"Sounds good. See you at home."

It wasn't home, Jacqui thought, walking to her car beside an atypically subdued Alice. Not for Mitch, and not for her. Neither of them needed to get too cozy with this setup. He'd be moving out soon—maybe even moving away, if he gave in to the restlessness she had sensed in him. She would do well to keep that eventuality in mind.

Chapter Four

Though she tried to convince him it wasn't necessary, Mitch helped Jacqui clear away the dinner dishes later that evening. Alice had gone to her room to take her almost-daily phone call from her mother in Hong Kong.

"Think she's telling her mother how unreasonable you and I were today not to let her hang out with a bunch of kids we don't know and ride in a car with an older boy?" Mitch asked.

Because Alice had been quiet during dinner and was still obviously irked that her spontaneous plans had been thwarted, Jacqui wasn't able to work up a smile in response to Mitch's half-teasing tone. "I hope not. But if she is, I hope her mother agrees with us."

"From what I've heard of her, she would. She's a long-distance parent, but Meagan said she's made it a point to back up Seth in whatever decisions he makes on Alice's behalf. At least in front of Alice. Seth and Colleen discuss her in private calls so they can present a united front to her."

Jacqui was already aware of that, of course, being a household insider, but she merely nodded. "I only met Colleen once, when she was in the state for a brief visit with Alice and her parents at Christmas, but it was obvious she loves Alice very much. She was very pleasant to me when she picked up Alice to take her to Heber Springs, where Colleen's parents live."

Colleen was tall, strikingly attractive, expensively fashionable. Although she had grown up in Arkansas, no traces of the South remained in her speech patterns— Jacqui would bet that had been a deliberate effort on Colleen's behalf. Rather than the slight drawl Jacqui had grown accustomed to hearing during the two years she'd lived in Little Rock, Colleen spoke rapidly, enunciating each syllable clearly. Her manner was courteous but somewhat brusque, hinting that her time was too valuable to waste on trivialities.

Jacqui supposed some people would be intimidated by the attorney, although she hadn't been. To her credit, Colleen hadn't been dismissive of her ex-husband's housekeeper, but instead had thanked her nicely for doing such a good job watching out for Alice when the other adults were occupied with their careers.

Seth's second wife was also a successful career woman, but other than that Meagan and Colleen couldn't be more different. Whereas Colleen was obsessed with career, Meagan's priority was family. The family she'd made with Seth and Alice, and the one in which she'd grown up, including her widowed mother and two younger siblings. Often she referred to Jacqui as a part of the family, a generous gesture that Jacqui appreciated even as she continually reminded herself that she was merely the housekeeper. If she were to fall and injure herself so that she was no longer able to fill the position, as had happened to the older woman who worked for Seth previously, they would hire someone to replace her, just as Jacqui had replaced Nina.

"Jacqui? Where have you drifted off to?"

She blinked up at Mitch, who was standing by the dishwasher and looking at her quizzically. Hastily placing the dish in her hand on the rack, she shook her head. "Sorry. I was just thinking about that little tiff with Alice. I've been lucky until this point, I guess. She's been absolutely no trouble at all every time I've watched her."

He shrugged. "If one quarrel and a chilly dinner are the worst you encounter, then you're lucky. I remember some of Madison's teen dramas. My folks were ready to lock her in the cellar a few times, I think. Guess it's a good thing we didn't actually have a cellar."

She smiled perfunctorily. "I guess every teen, no matter how generally well-behaved, hates hearing the word 'no.'"

He chuckled. "Oh, yeah. Didn't you have your share of teen rebellion when you were that age?"

Jacqui had rebelled every time her father had uprooted the family and drifted to another town where she and Olivia would be enrolled in yet another new school. Not that it had done her any good. Every time they'd moved, her parents had promised it would be the last time. They'd advised her to make the best of the life they led, to make new friends and experience new things—and to take care of her little sister while Mom and Dad were out doing odd jobs to support them.

The stabbing pain in her chest was familiar but still

agonizing. It seemed as though she'd thought of Olivia more than usual during the past few days. Partially, she supposed, because the anniversary of her sister's death was approaching—less than a month away now. And partially because the more Alice matured, the more she sometimes reminded Jacqui of Olivia—bright and inquisitive and imaginative, sweet-natured but with a stubborn streak that cropped up unexpectedly. Alice was only a few months younger than Olivia had been when she'd died.

There was no way that Alice would be riding in cars with teenage drivers on Jacqui's watch.

Determinedly, she buried the past deep in the back of her mind, though it had a nasty habit of clawing its way to the front when she was least prepared to handle it. Needing a change of subject, she turned the questioning to Mitch. "Have you given any more thought about a new place to live?"

He gave her a lopsided smile as he closed the dishwasher, his hand brushing hers with the movement. "Trying to get rid of me already?"

Something about his tone—or maybe that smile— made his teasing sound suspiciously like flirting. Probably it was just a habit of his—certainly nothing to take seriously.

When she didn't take him up on his verbal bait, he replied more seriously. "I talked to a few people today about some recommendations for Realtors and rental agents. And Mom gave me the name of a woman she knows who works part-time in real estate sales. I'll probably make a few calls tomorrow."

There was a distinct lack of enthusiasm in his voice. If he was thinking about looking for another rental, she didn't blame him for being less than excited about the search. She never liked doing that, either. It would be different when she started looking for a little place to buy, she promised herself. That lifelong ambition was going to be a joy to fulfill.

"Still looking for a place where you don't have to sign a lease?" she asked casually, her gaze on the counter she was wiping with a sponge.

Because she wasn't looking at him, she didn't see him shrug, but she heard the shift of fabric as his shoulder lifted in the negligent gesture. "Maybe. Or at least a place with a lenient lease-breaking policy."

She wrung out the towel and draped it over the sink to dry.

"My mom thinks I should buy a house," Mitch said with a chuckle. "She even suggested a couple of neighborhoods she thought suitable for me."

"I'm sure she's just trying to be helpful."

"Of course she is. Her first choice would be for me to buy Seth's house, which is still on the market. She pointed out how cozy it would be if I lived right across the street from my sister and brother-in-law."

"A little too cozy, maybe?"

He smiled. "Maybe. But I told her I'd think about it."

Outside in the backyard, Waldo barked. Jacqui glanced at the clock. "Alice usually goes out to play with him and give him a treat after dinner. He's probably wondering where she is."

"Does she usually talk this long with her mom?"

"No, not usually."

"Think she's still pouting?"

"Possibly."

Waldo barked again, the sound ending with a hint of a whine. Jacqui frowned. Alice was usually so attentive to her adored pet. She wouldn't punish Waldo because she was irked with the housekeeper; maybe Alice didn't realize how late it was getting.

She turned away from the sink. "I'll go check on her."

Saying he wanted to watch the news, Mitch headed for the den as Jacqui climbed the stairs toward Alice's room. Alice's door stood slightly ajar, and Jacqui could hear the teen laughing and giggling from the top of the stairs. It was not the voice she used with her mother, but rather the sillier, slangier tone that signified she was talking with one of her friends.

"He's so hot. And I think he likes me," she confided breathlessly to the person on the other side of the call. She giggled in response to whatever her friend said. "Yeah, he said he—"

Jacqui cleared her throat noisily.

"Uh, gotta go, Tiff. I'll call you later, okay?"

By the time Jacqui tapped lightly on the open door and stepped into the room, Alice had already disconnected the call.

"Everything okay?" Jacqui asked casually. "Waldo is looking for his evening treat."

Alice tossed back her curly hair and slid her phone in her pocket. "Okay, I'm on my way down. I was going to play with him for a while anyway before bed."

"He'll like that. Um, Alice?"

"Yes?"

Jacqui laced her fingers in front of her, mentally mapping a path to the conversational destination she hoped to achieve. "Milo *is* cute."

Alice's quick smile was both appreciative and suspicious. "Yeah, he's okay," she agreed a little too nonchalantly.

"But you know, of course, that he's too old to be hanging out with a fourteen-year-old. He should be flirting with girls his age—not girls almost four years younger. Just as your own friends should be fifteen and younger."

Alice exhaled sharply in exasperation. "Geez, Jacqui, we were just talking. But still, four years is hardly anything. Dad's almost four years older than Meagan and nobody has even mentioned it."

"It's different after you're eighteen. Trust me, those four years between fourteen and eighteen are a lot more significant than you think. Eighteen-year-olds have less supervision. They're driving and dating and other things you aren't quite ready for yet. You know your dad doesn't want you hanging out alone with boys just yet, and I agree with him. Don't be in too big a hurry to grow up and get involved with relationship drama. Have fun with your friends while you can still be just kids."

"I wasn't going out on a date with Milo. I just wanted to get a ride home with him. I'd have been perfectly safe. He said he's been driving for two whole years."

"It's still better if you don't ride alone with teen drivers just yet."

Jacqui didn't know how to explain that it was more than just the car ride—though that alone would have been enough for her to turn down Alice's request. She hadn't liked the way Milo had looked at sweet, naive Alice—and that would have been hard to explain to the girl. For one thing, Alice was as likely to be flattered by the attention as alarmed by the boy's intentions.

"You're totally overreacting," Alice muttered. "You don't even know Milo."

"I know a little more than you give me credit for,"

Jacqui replied evenly. "I've been around a while longer than you have, Alice."

Alice looked less than convinced. "I'm going down to play with Waldo."

Smothering a sigh, Jacqui thought about how glad she would be when Seth and Meagan returned from their trip. Between Mitch's unexpected stayover and Alice's out-of-the-blue hormonal rebellion, this week was turning out to be much more complicated than she had ever anticipated. She wanted to go back to being nothing more than the daytime housekeeper and part-time cook, efficient but basically invisible. Life was so much simpler that way, with way fewer obstacles waiting to trip her up.

Speaking of hazardous pitfalls...

She crossed paths with Mitch on the stairs as she headed down a few moments after Alice and he was on his way up. Though the stairway was plenty wide enough for both of them, it felt suddenly smaller when she and Mitch stood face to face.

"I was just going up to log some computer time in my room before bed," he explained with a smile. "Thought I'd do some real estate searches and answer a few emails."

"I'll be turning in early tonight, too." She was suddenly very tired, and she was aware that the exhaustion was more mental than physical. "I'll just finish up a few things in the kitchen and then I'll go to bed when Alice does. Is there anything else you need this evening?"

He chuckled. "There's that housekeeper voice again. No, Jacqui, there's nothing else I need tonight. And if there were, I'd get it for myself."

She nodded a little stiffly and took another step down. Because Mitch moved at the same time, and apparently misjudged her path, their shoulders collided. So much for having plenty of room on the stairway, she thought, pressing her hand to the wall for balance. Mitch caught her other arm as though to steady her.

"Sorry. You okay?"

"Of course. It was just a bump."

"My fault. I got distracted—wasn't looking where I was going."

As she recalled, he'd been looking at her face when he'd moved. Was he saying that she was a distraction to him? Or was she being as silly and flustered as Alice by an intriguing guy's attention?

Annoyed with herself, she started to move again, only to be detained by the light grasp Mitch still had on her forearm. She looked up at him with questioningly raised eyebrows. He stood now on the step below her, which brought their faces close to the same level. And he was looking directly at her mouth.

Self-consciously and without thinking, she moistened her lips. His eyes narrowed as though in response to what might have looked like an invitation, she realized hastily. Awkwardly, she took another step down, thinking she would hurry on her way, but all that did was bring her almost into his arms when he shifted on the step to accommodate her.

Mitch chuckled and caught her other shoulder with his free hand. "Hang on, we're going to knock each other down the stairs if we keep this up."

Pressing back against the wall, she tried to speak in the same light tone he'd used. "We do seem to be colliding a lot this weekend. It'll be a wonder if I don't cause you bodily damage before you find another place to stay."

His grin widened. "Is that a hint? Trying to run me off?"

Studying his devastatingly attractive smile through her lashes, she muttered, "I probably should be."

His smile faltered, but she slipped out of his grasp and moved quickly down the stairs before he could reply with whatever he might have said.

Some role model for Alice she was turning out to be, she thought in annoyance. When it came to a cute, completely unsuitable guy with a sexy smile, it seemed that neither of them had a lick of sense.

Brooks and Dunn wailed that "cowgirls don't cry" as Mitch skillfully wielded a number 69 Beaver blade on the adolescent hand he viewed through a magnifying glass. Mitch liked an eclectic selection of music while he worked; his amplified music player held an extensive collection of country, rock and alternative songs. The selection was varied enough that he didn't get bored with it and his assistants rarely complained, as they did about Dr. Burkett's vast library of polka tunes.

Seated at one side of the hand table, gloved and gowned, Mitch worked swiftly to repair the extensive damage that had been done to the boy's hand when a friend slammed a car door on it. He didn't want to take longer than necessary to make the repairs. More than two hours' use of the inflated tourniquet cutting off the blood supply to the hand increased the risk of long-term muscle damage.

His first assistant, a third-year surgical resident, stood at the other side of the hand table, watching the delicate procedure intently and eagerly and performing as much of the operation as Mitch allowed. A fourth-year medical student stood nearby, craning her head for a better view while doing her best to stay out of the way. At the end of the hand table, next to the vigilantly guarded sterile instrument tray, stood a surgical technician with whom Mitch had worked many long hours in various operations. They'd operated together so often that Brenda often knew what he needed before he even asked, handing over instruments in a smooth, practiced rhythm that made the process easier for both of them.

There wasn't a lot of time for chitchat during this procedure, as there was in some longer operations, but Brenda still asked at one point, "How's the house search coming along?"

"Haven't looked much yet," Mitch answered, taking a moment to stretch his neck muscles, which were tightening up from being held so long in the same position. "It's only been a few days."

"Still staying with your sister?"

"Well, in my sister's house. She's on a European vacation with her husband. Her stepdaughter and housekeeper are sharing the house with me for now."

"How old is the stepdaughter?"

"Fourteen."

"Challenging age."

Mitch thought of the chilly treatment Alice had given Jacqui during dinner last night. "You can say that again."

The boy on the table was only fifteen. And right-handed. Mitch turned his attention to the surgery again, determined that the kid would have full use of that hand again. Mitch loved his job—repairing young bodies damaged by accidents or ailments. The hours were long, the physical demands grueling, the emotional toll occasionally high—but he thrived on it. Sure, there were times when he wondered why he hadn't gone into

carpentry; it was a lot less stressful to repair broken
cabinets than broken bones, especially because he'd
chosen a pediatric specialty with so much at risk. But
those fleeting thoughts never lasted long. He was doing
what he'd been called to do.

Focused intently on the retractor he held, the resident
commented through his mask, "Living with a teenager
and a senior citizen is probably making you impatient
to get back into a place of your own."

Mitch spared a glance upward. "A senior citizen?"

The resident never looked up from his task. "The
housekeeper. Just an assumption."

"An incorrect one."

"Oops. My bad."

The medical student giggled, then subsided quickly
into silence, as though embarrassed to have called any
attention to herself. Mitch didn't even glance her way
but finished the operation without further conversation,
an image of Jacqui in the back of his mind. How would
she feel if she'd heard herself referred to as a senior
citizen?

Leaving the capable resident to close, he stood, taking care not to contaminate the sterile field around
the patient. He backed away from the table, his gloved
hands held above his waist. The medical student moved
up eagerly to take over first assistant position while
Brenda watched zealously to make sure the sterile field
remained unbroken.

Once out of range, Mitch dropped his arms and
arched his back to loosen the muscles there. He had
another surgery scheduled that afternoon, but he had an
hour free for lunch first. He would eat that meal at his
desk while he checked messages and returned calls.

The sandwich sat half eaten on his desk and the list of

phone numbers were held unheeded in his hand a short
while later. His thoughts had drifted to Jacqui again.
Specifically, he recalled that moment in the stairway
when their faces were on a level and her freshly moistened lips had been only a whisper away from his. He
could almost feel his hands on her arms as he'd steadied
her. Her body had been warm through her thin cotton
blouse, and he could only imagine how soft her skin
would be over the work-toned muscles beneath.

Definitely not a senior citizen.

He supposed he should find another place to live
soon. His growing attraction to Jacqui was likely to get
awkward if he stayed there much longer. As if it weren't
already awkward enough, at least for him.

Fortunately Alice's sulks didn't last through Monday.
By the time she and Jacqui had run errands together and
shared lunch at Alice's favorite Chinese buffet, the girl
was back in her usual good spirits. Neither of them mentioned the disagreement in the park. Jacqui wondered if
she should bring it up again, just as another opportunity
to make sure Alice understood what had been at stake,
but she decided to let it go.

Mitch had let her know he wouldn't be home from the
hospital until late that evening, so she and Alice shared
a quiet evening together. After a cooling swim in the
backyard pool, they spent a couple of hours knitting in
front of the TV. Jacqui finished some projects for her
friend's boutique while Alice worked on a pale-green
bear she would stuff with batting and add to her children's hospital gifts.

"It's kind of quiet around here without Mitch, isn't
it?" Alice remarked as they put away their yarns and
needles.

Jacqui smiled faintly. "A little."

"He's fun to be around. I'm glad he's my uncle now. And Madison's great as my new aunt, even if she has been so busy lately in her psychiatry residency that I've hardly seen her."

"You're very fortunate to have found such a nice bonus family." Alice didn't care for the term "stepfamily," so Jacqui was careful to avoid using it.

"I am lucky. I've got lots of family now. My dad. My mom. My grandparents in Heber Springs. My mom's sister and her family in Colorado—I don't see them much, but they're nice. My dad's father in Dallas. And now Meagan and her family. Mimi and Mitch and Madison."

Wondering a bit where this was going, Jacqui said lightly, "You forgot to mention Waldo."

Alice giggled. "Anyway, I'm glad I have a lot of family."

"Then I'm glad you're glad."

The girl smiled again.

"I know your grandparents are looking forward to seeing you this weekend." Beginning Friday, Alice would spend a few days with her maternal grandparents in Heber Springs. She would come home next Tuesday, two days before Seth and Meagan returned from their trip.

Her grandparents had hinted broadly that Alice should spend the entire two weeks with them while her dad and stepmother were away, but Alice had politely thanked them and reminded them about her obligations to her swim team. As it was, she would be missing a couple of practices to spend a few days with them. Jacqui knew Alice was fond of her grandparents, and she spent at least one weekend with them a month, but she had confided to Jacqui that sometimes there she missed her friends and activities at home.

Only then did it occur to Jacqui that she and Mitch would be alone in the house while Alice was with her grandparents. When they'd first made all these plans, Jacqui had assumed she would be returning to her apartment during those days, but that was before the leak had ruined her floors. She'd gone by that morning and the new carpeting still had not been installed. Her apartment was a mess at the moment, with her belongings piled on larger furniture and the floors stripped down to bare particle board, some of which had warped from water damage. The manager had assured her the repairs were being done as quickly as possible, but because several apartments had been damaged—and not all the other tenants had someplace else to stay—it was taking a while to get to them all.

She supposed it wouldn't be a problem sharing the house with Mitch for a few days. It wasn't as though he was here all that much. She would take great care to avoid any more awkward encounters like the one on the staircase. Staying in the background as the cook and housekeeper was the safest course—and one she fully intended to follow.

Or maybe he'd find someplace else to stay by then, she thought without much optimism.

"I guess it will be nice to stay with Grammy and Grampa—even though I was just there last month."

Hearing a distinct lack of enthusiasm in the girl's voice, Jacqui spoke cheerily, "You know how they love spending time with you. And your Grampa's going to take you fishing, isn't he? You always enjoy that."

Alice nodded. "Yeah, I like fishing. But I'd kind of like to stay here with you and Mitch, too. That was fun the other night—playing board games, I mean. And Mitch said maybe he'd take me to the hospital to deliver toys and visit with some of the kids this weekend, but I told him I couldn't because I'm staying with my grandparents."

"I'm sure he'll take you another time."

"Yeah, he said he would. But still—"

"Your grandparents would be very disappointed if you cancel your visit with them, Alice."

"I won't cancel," Alice promised. "I know that would hurt their feelings. But don't do anything too much fun with Uncle Mitch while I'm gone, okay?" she added with a teasing smile.

Jacqui forced a smile. "I wouldn't worry about that. Your uncle will probably hang out with his friends again when he's not working, and I have a few tentative plans. My friend Alexis and I have been trying to get together for lunch and shopping, and we're hoping our schedules will both be clear this weekend."

Alexis Johnson was one of Jacqui's few good friends in Little Rock, outside the family she worked for. They'd met in a four-week vegetarian cooking class they had both taken last year and had gotten together occasionally since. Alexis traveled a lot in her job as a flight attendant and was involved in several organizations that took a great deal of her time, but she and Jacqui tried to get together whenever they could for a few hours of girl talk and relaxation. On the surface, the friends seemed to have little in common. Alexis was very much into fashion and appearance, whereas Jacqui had only passing interest in clothes and shoes, but they'd been drawn together by similar senses of humor and a mutual fondness for Indian food.

Looking vaguely surprised, Alice tilted her head in

Jacqui's direction. Was the girl having a hard time envisioning that Jacqui had a life outside the Llewellyn family? Okay, maybe she didn't do much other than work, Jacqui admitted silently, but she did have a few friends and hobbies of her own.

"I thought maybe you and Mitch would do something while I'm gone. You know, like go out for dinner together or something." Alice's tone was just a little too nonchalant, which made Jacqui frown suspiciously. Surely the girl wasn't matchmaking?

"If your uncle wants me to make dinner for him, I'd be happy to do so," she answered evenly. "That's part of my job."

"I didn't mean for your job," Alice insisted, raising Jacqui's suspicions even further. "I mean—well, uncle Mitch is cute, right? And he's pretty close to your age. Not even as much different as Milo and me... even though I still don't think four years is all that much," she added in a grumble.

Jacqui had no intention of getting into another debate about whether it was appropriate for Alice to hang out with an almost-eighteen-year-old boy—it could only lead to another bout of sulks because Jacqui had no intention of changing her mind. Nor did she want to get into a discussion about why she and Mitch were not a good match despite being single adults of close to the same age.

"Would you carry these empty teacups to the kitchen for me, please?" she requested, folding away her knitting as she spoke. "It's getting late. If you want to play with Waldo a little before bedtime, you'd better go on out."

But Alice wasn't quite finished with their conversation. "It's just...well, like we said, it's nice to have family."

"I have family, Alice," Jacqui countered gently. She supposed it was touching that Alice worried about her being alone, even if it was somewhat awkward. "My parents are still living. I talk with them occasionally, even if we aren't as close as you are with your parents."

"But you really like our family, right? I mean, Uncle Mitch and Meagan and Madison and Mimi and my dad and all. And they all really like you, too."

"That's nice to hear. Now go play with Waldo."

"I just thought…maybe…if you were dating someone yourself, you'd be a little more…you know, relaxed about things."

Jacqui nearly sighed in response to the muttered remark. So it all came back to Alice's new crush on Milo Lemon. So much for the sweet motives Jacqui had just attributed to the wily teen.

She glanced at her watch. "You have half an hour to play with your dog before bedtime. Keep procrastinating and you'll find out just how unrelaxed I can be."

Alice sighed gustily and snatched up the empty teacups. "Fine. Be all grouchy. Just because I wanted you to be happy and stuff."

Torn between exasperation and wry amusement, Jacqui merely motioned her out of the room.

Chapter Five

Jacqui found herself preparing dinner Tuesday evening for Mitch's family. It had all begun with a call from LaDonna early that morning. LaDonna had said that her sisters-in-law wanted to come see Meagan's house sometime that day. They were disappointed, LaDonna said, that Meagan was out of town during their visit, but that was their own fault.

"I told them when they called to arrange this visit that Meagan would be out of town on her belated honeymoon trip during this time, but they said it was the best week for them to come," she said into the phone, her voice low so as not to carry to her guests in another room. "They really have no reason to complain about missing Meagan."

"I'm sure she would have loved to see them, too."

"They would like to come see her house. Don't know why, when she's not even there, but they've got it in their heads they want to come by. And to be honest, I'm running out of things to do to entertain them. Do you mind a visit sometime later today, Jacqui?"

"Of course not. It's your daughter's home—you're certainly welcome here."

"Thank you. All we've done the past few days is drive around and dine out or eat here and I just don't know what else to do with them. They seem to only enjoy eating and chatting and riding in the car," LaDonna added with a wry laugh.

Jacqui spoke impulsively, "Why don't you plan to bring them here for dinner? I'm sure Alice would love playing hostess at a dinner party for her aunts."

LaDonna had jumped on that offer eagerly, despite her token protests that it would be too much trouble for Jacqui to put a dinner party together that quickly. Reminding LaDonna that she would be making dinner for herself and Alice and Mitch anyway, Jacqui assured her it would be no trouble to add a few guests. They might as well invite Madison, too, and make it a family gathering.

Jacqui knew it was a little strange that there would be a dinner party in Meagan's home when Meagan wasn't even there, but she was confident Meagan and Seth would be more amused than annoyed. Both were well accustomed to Meagan's aunt's eccentricities. And both would do anything to assist LaDonna with anything she needed.

Doreen O'Connor and Kathleen Baker were twins in their mid-sixties. Jacqui had met them only once, at Meagan and Seth's wedding, and that had been only a fleeting encounter. Although they looked very much alike, Jacqui didn't think they were identical twins. She saw a few differences in them that helped her tell them apart when LaDonna reintroduced them that evening. LaDonna did not refer to Jacqui as her daughter's house- keeper but as a friend of the family. Jacqui didn't bother to correct her, even though she certainly wasn't embar- rassed by her job title. She figured the aunts knew her role in the family.

"And here," LaDonna added with a warm smile, "is my new granddaughter, Alice."

The sisters greeted Alice pleasantly, urging her to call them Aunt Doreen and Aunt Kathleen. With her usual ebullience, Alice was soon chattering away to them as if she'd known them for years rather than having met them only once before. She led them off on a tour of the house before dinner. It didn't take her long to charm them with her excellent company manners.

Mitch's sister Madison arrived shortly after LaDonna and the twins. She made a little face at Jacqui, who had opened the door for her. "Sorry Mom roped you into this," she murmured. "Is there anything I can do to help?"

"It's no trouble," Jacqui assured her honestly. "I al- ways enjoy cooking for a dinner party. Everyone is gath- ered in the living room. I have everything under control in the kitchen, so why don't you join your family?"

"Is Mitch here yet?"

"Not yet. He just called to say he's running a little late and for us to start dinner without him if we need to."

Smoothing her breeze-ruffled blond hair, Madison chuckled. "The surgeon's life. That's why I chose psy- chiatry. Shorter hours."

Madison always teased about that, but Jacqui didn't believe it any more than Madison's family did. During the one-year-plus that she'd known Meagan's younger sister, it had become clear to Jacqui that Madison was the most empathetic of the Baker siblings. Meagan and Mitch had both chosen surgery because they enjoyed the challenge of fixing something physical that was broken. Madison was more interested in soothing mental and emotional pain, whether triggered by chemical imbalances or life experiences.

Jacqui was just putting the finishing touches on individual Caprese salads when LaDonna wandered into the kitchen. "Can I help you with anything, dear?"

"No, thank you, LaDonna. Everything is almost ready."

The other woman had insisted from the beginning of their acquaintance that Jacqui should call her by her first name rather than the more formal Mrs. Baker. Fifty-nine and widowed for several years, LaDonna Baker eschewed stuffiness and formality, treating everyone with the same easy warmth. A CPA, she had gone back to work four days a week as a bookkeeper after the death of her mother last year. Like her three offspring, LaDonna didn't seem to be content unless she was gainfully employed. She had taken a week's vacation from her job to entertain her sisters-in-law.

"If you think everyone is ready to eat, I can start serving. Mitch should be here soon, but he didn't want anyone to have to wait for him."

"He works too hard. All my children do." LaDonna shook her head in slight disapproval. Something about her expression reminded Jacqui very much of Meagan. Both Meagan and Madison favored their fair, slender mother. Although Mitch bore some family resemblance, Jacqui assumed he must look more like his late father.

Responding to LaDonna's comment, Jacqui nodded in agreement. "Yes, they do."

"And so do you. You've had your hands full taking care of Alice and Mitch while Meagan and Seth are away, haven't you? And I've added to your work by bringing my sisters-in-law for dinner."

"I didn't mind at all."

"I can't tell you how much I appreciate this. I'm running out of ways to entertain them," LaDonna confided in a murmur. "They get bored easily and want me to keep coming up with new things for us to do. At least a dinner party here is something different."

Jacqui chuckled. "Then we'll make sure they're entertained."

She honestly didn't mind helping out with entertaining the women, even if it was just to serve them dinner. Jacqui had grown very fond of LaDonna during the past year. LaDonna had been nothing but gracious to her, and Jacqui admired the way LaDonna had welcomed Alice into her family. Jacqui doubted any future biological grandchildren would be treated with any more interest and affection from their "Mimi."

Jacqui had worried about LaDonna at the end of last year. Already saddened by the untimely loss of her husband, LaDonna had worn herself almost to the ends of her physical and emotional limits caring for her dying mother. She was still too thin, in Jacqui's private opinion, but she seemed to be recovering now from her grief and stress. Her job had helped distract her from that trying time. As had her joy in her three children and her new granddaughter.

"Don't you even think about staying in here and serving while we're eating," the older woman warned with a shake of her finger. "You are eating with us, right?"

The formal dining table seated eight, so there was room for Jacqui to join them, even though she would have been just as happy to eat at the breakfast-nook table where the casual family usually dined. But because LaDonna had already insisted she join them when they'd first discussed a menu for the evening, Jacqui knew there was no use in demurring. "Yes, I'll join you. I can serve and eat at the same time."

LaDonna nodded in approval. "Good."

Jacqui slipped a pan of seasoned salmon fillets and a separate dish of asparagus spears into the oven to bake while they ate their salads; she had a Dijon-dill sauce chilling in the fridge to spoon over the fish she would serve with herbed rice and the lemon-sprinkled asparagus. She'd long since learned that careful timing was the secret to success with a dinner party, especially if she was eating and serving.

Mitch rushed into the dining room just as Jacqui finished setting the salads in front of their guests. "Sorry I'm late," he said a little breathlessly. "I had a procedure that took longer than I expected this afternoon."

Welcoming him warmly, his adoring mother and aunts presented cheeks for him to kiss. Grinning, he rounded the table, planting noisy kisses on those cheeks, then on his sister's and niece's for good measure.

Alice giggled. "You didn't kiss Jacqui."

Jacqui forced her smile to remain in place even as she shot Alice a look. "That's not necessary," she said lightly. "I'm not family."

Chuckling, Mitch leaned down to press a smacking kiss to her too-warm cheek. "Of course you are," he said heartily. "You came with the package."

She busied herself with her salad as he took his seat. Apparently taking pity on her, Madison spoke quickly, asking Alice about her swim team, which started the conversation in a new direction.

Grateful, Jacqui glanced Madison's way, but because Mitch was seated next to his younger sister, she accidentally caught his eyes instead. He winked at her, making her look quickly back down at the tomatoes, mozzarella and basil on her plate. Although this was her favorite salad, suddenly she found it difficult to swallow.

Jacqui fit in very well with his family, Mitch mused during the scrumptious dessert that followed her excellent meal. But she seemed to be doing everything she could to remain separate from them. She jumped up constantly during the meal to wait on everyone, serving from the left and removing from the right with the efficiency of a banquet server rather than an attentive hostess. She might as well have worn a name tag identifying her as an employee of the household. He wasn't sure how, exactly, his mom had roped her into this, but Jacqui handled a last-minute dinner party with the same efficient aplomb with which she did all the responsibilities of her job.

To give them credit, his aunts didn't treat her any differently than they did any of the others at this somewhat unconventional dinner party. With their usual curiosity—okay, nosiness—they eagerly included Jacqui in the series of personal questions they threw at Mitch, Madison and even Alice. Jacqui, he noted, was good at giving polite nonanswers—so skilled at it that it was only later one realized she hadn't really divulged much information at all.

"Do you want to be a lawyer like your father or a doctor like your stepmother and her brother and sister?" Kathleen asked Alice during the dessert. "Or maybe a CPA like your new grandmother?"

"Both my parents are lawyers," Alice replied, carefully including her mother in the list. "But I want to be an orthodontist."

"An orthodontist?" Doreen smiled. "That's not something you hear very often from a girl your age."

Alice grinned, displaying the braces she'd been wearing for just more than a year. "I've had plenty of chances to watch what my orthodontist does. It looks interesting. And I like the thought of making people feel better about their smiles."

"That's very nice," Kathleen approved. "A good reason to go into a field. That's why all LaDonna's children went into medicine, I'm sure—to help people. Not for the money."

Madison laughed wryly. "You really must have stronger reasons to go into medicine than money. In my opinion, no amount of pay is a good-enough incentive alone to get through medical school. There are a lot less stressful ways to make a decent salary."

Alice giggled. "Dad and Meagan are always play-arguing about which is harder, medical school or law school."

"Medical school," Mitch and Madison said in unison.

"That's hardly fair," Mitch's mother commented. "Seth isn't here to defend his side of the argument."

"Wouldn't matter. He'd be wrong," Mitch stated firmly, making Alice giggle again.

"I wish they were here," Doreen remarked with exaggerated wistfulness. "We haven't seen them since their wedding. I was sure we told them then when we'd be here for a visit."

LaDonna shook her head firmly. "You said then that you were thinking about coming in September. It was only after Meagan and Seth made their travel arrangements for Europe that you switched the date to this week. The change worked fine for my schedule, but Meagan and Seth couldn't just cancel or reschedule their one chance at a belated honeymoon trip."

Mitch knew his mom would get chippy if her sisters-in-law continued to criticize Meagan and Seth, even in subtle jabs. He was relieved when Madison, ever the peacemaker, spoke up quickly.

"Jacqui, this cake is absolutely decadent. Sin on a plate but worth every calorie."

Mitch saw the flash of pride in Jacqui's eyes before she replied in a stage whisper, "Don't tell any of the others, but it's actually a healthy recipe. It's low-fat, low-sugar. Applesauce and crushed pineapple are what make it so moist and sweet."

"You're kidding! Then maybe I should have a second slice," Madison teased. "Really, it's delicious."

The others all added their compliments to the dessert, although Mitch noticed Kathleen, the pickiest eater in the family, now eyed the cake with a little more suspicion. Both the twins were heavy, but Kathleen was the bread-and-sweet fanatic, refusing to even consider gentle suggestions that she should make healthy changes in her diet. He found it amusing that she'd been wolfing down the rich-tasting dessert with enthusiasm until she'd heard it wasn't actually so bad for her.

Jacqui really was an excellent cook. He'd heard Meagan and Seth comment about how much they enjoyed the meals she prepared for them. Seth's former housekeeper had been more of a traditional meat-and-potatoes chef, leaning heavily on Tex-Mex recipes. Although Seth had confided that he'd loved Nina's cooking, he had also admitted that Jacqui's lighter touch with fresh vegetables and fruits and leaner meats was a much healthier diet for him and his daughter.

Jacqui took as much pride in her work as any of them did, Mitch mused. Yet he suspected she was as aware as he was that housekeeping hadn't been listed in the potential careers for Alice. It was a perfectly respectable and worthwhile job, but he had to admit it wasn't one that immediately came to mind. He would like to know more about how Jacqui had ended up in this particular career—and if she had any plans to do anything different in the future—but she was so darned skittish about personal questions.

Was it that evasiveness that made him so increasingly curious about her? Was she simply an intriguing puzzle he was drawn to solve? He'd always liked a challenge. But it felt as though there was more to his attraction to Jacqui. Had been from the start. Even though she hadn't given him even a hint of encouragement.

Well, not specifically, anyway. He thought of that moment when their paths had crossed on the stairs and he'd gotten the feeling she felt some sparks between them, too. Had that been entirely in his own imagination?

"Your mother pointed out Seth's house that's for sale across the street, Mitchell," Doreen remarked, seemingly out of the blue. He felt a muscle tense in the back of his neck. "It's a very nice place," she added. "You should consider buying it for yourself now that you need a new home."

Kathleen nodded energetically. "It's lovely to live close to your sister, Mitchell. Doreen and I have never lived more than ten miles apart in our lives, and we don't regret it for one moment."

"Twelve miles."

Kathleen turned to her twin with a frown. "What?"

"The house I lived in with Gerald— That was my second late husband, Jacqui, God rest his soul. Anyway, that house was twelve miles from the town house you lived in then. You told Mitchell we'd never lived more than ten miles apart."

"Oh, good grief, Doreen, there's no need to get that specific. What does it matter if it was ten or twelve?"

"Well, you said ten."

Though he'd hoped the tiff would distract her, Kathleen turned determinedly back to Mitch. "The point is, it's nice to live close to your family, even if they drive you crazy sometimes," she added pointedly. "I think it's a sign that the other house is still available just when your apartment burned down."

Kathleen had always been led by "signs" and "feelings." Despite her own resistance to any well-intentioned guidance toward herself, she didn't mind giving frequent advice to others, something the rest of the family tolerated indulgently. Most of the time.

Although her twin had been widowed twice, Kathleen had never married. She claimed she'd had a lifelong "feeling" that she was meant to stay single and in a position to offer helpful, objective advice to others on maintaining their marriages and raising their children.

Mitch had always figured that for the sake of the twins' relationship, it was just as well Doreen had never had children with either of her husbands. Kathleen would have certainly been compelled to give her sister guidance on how to raise them, which Doreen would probably have resented eventually. As it was, both Kathleen and Doreen had been active, if long-distance, observers of their brother's family life, asking questions and tendering parenting critiques whenever they visited. Mitch wondered if his dad had chosen to move from his childhood home in St. Louis to take a position at the university in Little Rock specifically to get a little farther away from his lovable but meddling older sisters.

He didn't voice that pondering aloud, of course. "I said I would think about it."

"A man—a doctor, to boot—should have his own house," Doreen commented.

"And a family to fill it with," Kathleen added with a sage nod. "You're over thirty now, Mitchell. Time passes before you realize it."

He kept his smile in place with an effort. "I'll keep that in mind, Aunt Kathleen. Thanks."

He shot a glance at Madison, silently urging her to change the subject. But she merely gave him an exaggeratedly innocent smile in return, probably glad the aunts weren't quizzing her about her life choices instead.

"Even if you don't buy Seth's house—and I can't imagine why you aren't jumping at that chance, he'd probably make you a good deal, being family and all. Where was I? Oh, yes, even if you don't buy that one, you should consider buying or building rather than renting. Much better investment of your money."

"Thanks for the advice, Aunt Doreen." He searched his mind quickly for a change of topic. "How's your sciatica been lately?"

"Don't get her started on that," Kathleen cut in quickly. "I agree with her on the buying versus renting. I've done both, you know, and when I was younger, I preferred owning my own place. Now that I'm older, it's just too much upkeep. The senior living apartments Doreen and I are in now are perfect for us. But because you have no plans to leave Little Rock, you might as well invest in a nice house where you can settle down and raise a family."

Mitch noticed that Jacqui was focusing studiously on her tea mug, as if reading futures in the dregs there. He wondered whimsically if she could see his.

Kathleen's eyes narrowed on his face when he didn't immediately respond to her comments. Another one of her "feelings"? "You aren't planning on leaving Little Rock, are you, Mitchell?"

"I get tempting offers from other places occasionally, but I don't have any specific plans to move," he replied lightly. "I just like keeping my options open, you know?"

His mother made a funny little sound, as if she, too, had heard a hint of restlessness in his voice that was new to her. "Mitch? You're thinking about leaving Arkansas?"

Had she really just paled a shade at the very possibility? He tugged lightly at the collar of his white shirt. He'd left the top two buttons unfastened, but it still felt as if it had just tightened somehow. "I said I have no real plans to do so, Mom. I'm just trying to make the best decisions for my future. It hasn't even been a week since my place burned down and I've been pretty busy at work since. You can't expect me to buy a house in only a couple of days."

Taking pity either on him or their mother, Madison interceded then. "Tell our aunts about the trip you're taking to Peru, Mitch."

He appreciated the effort, but he wasn't sure that was the best change of subject. His mother was already fretting about whether he would be safe on that trek with his buddies, even though he'd assured her it was not a dangerous trip. Certainly not on the level of climbing Mt. Everest or some of the other risky adventure vacations he could have taken. Downplaying even a hint of

peril, he gave his aunts a quick description of the trip
his friends had mapped out for a five-day trek to Machu
Picchu.

"I'm leaving in about six weeks with some friends.
I'm really looking forward to it," he added candidly. "I
need the break."

He answered several questions about his plans,
promising everyone again that he would be perfectly
safe. Seeing that his mom was looking a little tense
again, he was relieved when Alice launched into a chatty
description of her visit to Europe with her mother the
previous summer. Mitch figured Alice had been quiet
for a while to let the others talk, probably in an attempt
to not monopolize the conversation, but now the pent-
up words tumbled out of her. He was selfishly pleased
when the aunts began to question her instead of grilling
him about his plans. Ostensibly, they were prompting
Alice for more information about her vacation, but he
knew they really wanted to hear more details about the
woman who'd previously been married to their niece's
new husband.

Even if Alice suspected their motives, which he
doubted, she didn't mind. She enjoyed talking about
her mother, making it clear she had few resentments
toward the attorney who had chosen a career path
that had taken her so very far from her only daughter.
Seth really had done a good job of keeping the lines of
communication open between his daughter and his ex-
wife, Mitch mused. And Meagan supported that agenda
completely.

Which only proved, he thought, that families didn't
have to live right next door to each other to remain
close and connected. Not that he was planning to leave
any time soon—but if that was what it took to fill that

growing emptiness inside him, then he liked to think he could do so without sacrificing what he had here.

Looking around the table at the smiling faces surrounding him—his family—he paused on Jacqui. She was smiling, too, as she paid attention to Alice's stories, which she'd probably heard many times before. But there was an expression in her eyes that looked all too familiar to him. As if she, too, was still looking for something she couldn't quite define.

Or was he letting himself be overly influenced by Aunt Kathleen's "feelings"? To be perfectly honest, he had no idea what Jacqui was thinking. Which only made her all the more intriguing to him.

"That was very nice of you to cook for my aunts this evening," Mitch said to Jacqui much later that night. Alice was already in bed, and Jacqui had been checking to make sure the back kitchen door was locked before turning in herself when Mitch wandered into the room.

She hadn't seen him for the past couple hours since his family had left and he'd excused himself to do some work at the desk in his room. She'd spent those hours cleaning up from the impromptu party, watching Alice swim and play with Waldo for a little while, then completing her latest knitting project for a short while after Alice had gone upstairs. Maybe she'd still been wired from the somewhat hectic day; only now, at just after eleven, did she feel relaxed enough to attempt sleep.

Because she'd already turned off all the lights except the night-light over the stove, the room lay in deep, hushed shadows. Even Waldo had gone to bed, judging from the silence in the backyard. A more fanciful person might imagine that she and Mitch were the only two people on the street still awake at this hour.

"You did an amazing job putting together a dinner party on such short notice. The food was excellent, as always."

She had a weakness for compliments about her cooking. She did try very hard to prepare good food that other people enjoyed eating. "I'm glad you liked it. And it wasn't much trouble. I didn't mind at all helping your mom out."

"I could tell she was grateful. She already liked you, but now you're her new best friend," he said with a chuckle.

She smiled. "I like her, too."

Her smile faded when she tried to think of a tactful way to phrase her next question. "Does your mother look—well, healthy to you, lately? I mean, it's probably a silly question with all three of her children being doctors, but she's just so thin."

Although he looked a little surprised, he shook his head. "It's not a silly question. I appreciate your concern for her. She's been a little stressed with the aunts here visiting, but I think she's fine. She's always been slim, and she tends to forget to eat when she has a lot going on. Remember how thin she got that last month of my grandmother's life? We were all fussing at her then."

Jacqui did remember. She hadn't seen as much of LaDonna then because that had been before Seth and Meagan married, but she had seen enough to be concerned. Not even quite sixty yet, LaDonna looked young for her age normally, but that sad and stressful time had taken a toll on her. Since Seth and Meagan's wedding, she'd looked happier and healthier—but the past couple of times Jacqui had seen LaDonna, she'd thought she noticed a change again. And not for the better.

Maybe she was just overreacting to a couple of pounds' weight loss. As much as Jacqui liked all of this family, she supposed she was a little too concerned about their well-being. Her job was simply to take care of this house and watch out for Alice occasionally. And if none of LaDonna's three physician offspring were concerned about their mother's health, then who was she to question their judgment?

"I'll remind her to take care of herself," Mitch said. "That's her problem, you know. She's always so busy caring for everyone else, she forgets to see to her own needs."

Jacqui smiled wryly. "And she raised three caregivers. What a surprise."

He chuckled. "Maybe she influenced us a bit."

"You think?"

He nodded, his smile fading. "Actually, Meagan is the one who's most like her, and she almost paid dearly for that last year. She discounted some pain she was experiencing as intense but ordinary monthly cramps. She was too busy with work to pay close attention to her own symptoms, and by the time she did, she needed emergency surgery. I can't remember if that was before you met her."

"I met her while she was on medical leave to recover from that operation," she reminded him. "She's the one who originally interviewed me as a favor to Seth. He was going through a busy time at the law office and she had some time off, so it worked out for both of them for her to screen some applicants for the housekeeping position."

"And she highly recommended you, as I understand

it. With a strong endorsement from Alice, who'd also met you that first day and decided you were the perfect candidate."

"I was grateful to both of them," she answered candidly. "Without their support, I'm not sure Seth would have even looked at my application twice. He had in mind someone older and more experienced, like his previous housekeeper. She'd been with him for several years and still would be if she hadn't fallen and broken her leg. I know they stay in touch, although he said she seems happy living in Mississippi near her daughter now."

"We're all glad Meagan urged Seth to hire you," Mitch murmured.

Suddenly the kitchen seemed shadowy and intimate again, their lightly casual conversation morphing into something a little different. She swallowed and backed a half step away from him. He wasn't really standing all that close, but she needed that extra bit of distance.

Maybe he sensed that she was more than ready to end this line of conversation. "I guess I'll turn in. Good night, Jacqui."

"Good night."

He paused in the doorway with a frown. "Mitch."

Her eyebrows rose. "I beg your pardon?"

"Good night, *Mitch*. You seem to go out of your way to avoid calling me by name."

So he'd noticed that, had he? It would have been so much easier to keep a firm distance between them if he would just allow her to call him Dr. Baker. "Good night, Mitch," she said.

His smile made it clear that the invisible barrier she'd so carefully erected had just shrunk considerably, despite her efforts. "Good night, Jacqui," he said again. "Sweet dreams."

She swallowed a groan when he turned and sauntered away. She didn't even want to think about the dreams that might plague her that night.

Chapter Six

Mitch wasn't quite sure how to ask Jacqui a big favor Saturday morning during breakfast. Because he'd been busy at work and had a full schedule for the past few evenings, he'd seen little of her since their conversation in the kitchen late Tuesday evening. He hadn't come in until after ten last night, only to find a note from her saying she'd turned in early and he could help himself to the leftover pie in the fridge if he was hungry for a late-night snack.

Forgoing the pie, he'd gone to bed. Even as tired as he'd been after a hectic week, it had taken him a while to go to sleep. He'd lay there wondering if she'd deliberately avoided seeing him that evening because they didn't have Alice as a buffer between them. Alice had left Friday morning for her extended weekend with her maternal grandparents. Jacqui had assured him there would be no differences in household routines while

Alice was away, but it hadn't escaped his notice that she'd gone up to her room earlier than was her usual habit last night.

She had greeted him this morning the way she always did, with a polite smile and a hot, healthy breakfast. At least she didn't try to avoid eating with him this time. She sat at the opposite side of the table with her bowl of steel-cut oats and fresh fruit.

He glanced past her to the glass patio doors, through which he could see Waldo wolfing down the food in his big stainless steel bowl. "Looks like Waldo's having his breakfast, too."

She chuckled. "He didn't get the kisses Alice gives him before breakfast, but I did rub his ears and throw the ball for him a few times."

Kisses before breakfast sounded pretty good to Mitch. Pushing an all-too-appealing image out of his mind, he cleared his throat. "That dog's got a pretty good life."

"He does, doesn't he? He's lucky Seth insisted Alice choose a dog from the local animal shelter when she decided she wanted a pet for her thirteenth birthday. She's been hinting strongly lately that she wants a cat, but Seth has been holding firm that the family is too busy to pay enough attention to more than one pet at a time."

He could understand that. As much as he liked animals, he hadn't had time to devote to a pet since he'd left high school. "You seem to enjoy Waldo. Ever thought of having a pet of your own?"

She shrugged. "I never had one growing up, but I might like to have a small dog, or maybe a cat, when I buy my own house."

He was always interested in those passing mentions of her past, but he'd learned not to follow up with questions that only made her shut down. Instead, he focused on her future plans. "You're buying a house?"

"Oh, not yet," she answered quickly. "I'm saving for a down payment. I'd like to have my own house someday, but it won't be for a couple of years yet."

That seemed as good a segue as any for the favor he wanted to request of her. "Do you have plans for today?"

She paused momentarily in reaching for her coffee cup, as if trying to figure out why he'd asked. "Not specifically," she answered after that almost imperceptible hesitation. "I had tentative plans to have lunch with a friend, but that fell through when something came up she had to attend to. So, I thought I might tackle some window washing this afternoon."

"It's Saturday. You don't normally work on Saturdays, do you?"

"Not every Saturday. Sometimes I come over for a couple of hours when the family needs help with something."

"You probably wouldn't be staying here this weekend with Alice gone if you didn't feel you have to cook for me."

"Not just that," she corrected him. "The new carpet is being installed in my apartment Monday. I could stay there if I had nowhere else to go, I suppose, but it's easier for all involved for me to stay out of the way."

"You don't really want to wash windows today, do you?"

She eyed him suspiciously. "You have something else in mind for me to do?"

Resisting all the inappropriate responses that popped into his head, he gave her what he hoped was a winning and totally innocuous smile. "Actually, I do. How would you like to help me look for a place to live?"

Her brows rose. Maybe he hadn't phrased that very well. "I need to spend today looking at apartments and houses," he explained. "I have a list of several possibilities and I've made arrangements to see them, but it's really not something I want to do alone."

Jacqui frowned a little. "Why would you want me to go with you?"

"If I go alone, I'm going to get bored and overwhelmed and I'll either just pick one to get it over with—which could be a big mistake—or I'll get distracted by something else and I'll end the day no closer to having a new place than I am now. It's pretty much what I did last time I had to find a place. I just grabbed the first available rental. Fortunately, that worked out pretty well—until the ditz burned it down," he added in a grumble.

"Why would you get bored looking for a place to live?" she asked in apparent bewilderment.

He shrugged. "Lack of interest to start with, I guess. I mean, it's not like I'm home all that much, wherever I stash my stuff. I'm either at the hospital or some professional function or at my mom's or hanging out with friends when I get the chance. I know I need to find someplace quick. Seth and Meagan don't want a permanent houseguest. My aunts are leaving today, so I could stay with Mom for a while, but that doesn't seem right, either. Work's going to be hectic for the next few weeks while I try to clear my calendar for my trip to Peru, so I should take advantage of this free weekend to make living arrangements."

"But why would you want me to go along?"

"As I said, I'd like the company. Objective opinions. Madison was going with me, but she called very early this morning and had to cancel because something came up. You always seem so practical and logical about things. I would value your input. I'm sure looking at apartments and houses is hardly your idea of a good time, but I'd buy you a very nice lunch to make it worth your while," he added hopefully.

If it bothered her that she hadn't been the first person he'd asked to accompany him, she gave no sign. He wondered if that actually made it easier for her to accept—making the whole suggestion less personal. More impulsive. It was hard to guess the thoughts that flashed through her mind before she finally replied. "It does sound more interesting than washing windows."

He chuckled. "Thank you for that, anyway."

"If I go, I should warn you that I tend to say what I think. I tell my friends not to ask my opinion about anything unless they really want the truth about what I'm thinking."

"That's exactly what I want you to do," he assured her, taking encouragement from the warning rather than the opposite. "You wouldn't let me sign anything just to get the whole process over with more quickly, would you?"

She shook her head in what might have been exasperation. "Honestly, you'd think a competent surgeon would take important decisions like this more seriously."

He grinned sheepishly. "I do take work decisions seriously. It's other stuff I have trouble concentrating on. Especially something I don't really want to do. It wasn't my choice, you know? I feel like I'm having to do something because of the ditz's stupidity, not because it was something I decided on my own to do right now."

She studied his face for a few moments in silence and

he wondered what she saw there that seemed to intrigue her. "Do you feel like a lot of your decisions are made for you?" she asked after that pause.

Caught off guard by the question, he answered without stopping to think. "For almost all of my life."

Then, because that sounded whiney and ungrateful—neither of which suited him—he chuckled lightly and said, "But isn't that the way it is for just about everyone?"

She merely shrugged, then asked, "What time do you want to leave?"

He glanced at his watch. "Whenever you're ready."

She stood to carry her empty bowl to the sink. "I assume this is a casual-dress outing, so all I have to do is grab my bag."

Her yellow-and-white knit top and jeans looked fine to him. *Very* fine, he added mentally, surreptitiously admiring the way the jeans hugged her slender bottom. He lifted his gaze quickly before she turned back toward him, not wanting her to catch him checking out her backside.

"I'm ready, too," he said, rising with his own empty breakfast dishes. "I'll get the list and meet you at the door."

"Fine."

If she was looking forward to the outing—or dreading it—there was no way to tell from her placid expression. He couldn't help wondering if there was anyone who knew Jacqui well enough to read her emotions when she made an effort to hide them.

Mitch had predicted Jacqui would take the house hunt seriously—she seemed to take most things seriously—but he was rather amused by how intently she went about the search. During the drive to the first apartment, she helped him make out a quick checklist of the things that were important to him. Location, price, privacy, parking. Because he wasn't committed to either renting or buying, they were looking at a selection of apartments, condos and houses.

"There's always Seth's house," he said as he parked in the lot of the first apartment complex. "I'm sure he'd offer me a good deal. I know there have been a few nibbles on it the past week, one fairly serious offer, so if I take that one, I'll have to grab it soon."

She tilted her head his way to study his face as she reached for her door handle. "I don't think you should buy Seth's house."

Apparently she was following through on her warning that she would tell him exactly what she thought today.

"Yeah? How come?" he asked, genuinely curious about her reasoning.

She lifted one shoulder slightly. "You aren't excited about it. It's something you feel obligated to consider because your mom likes the idea and because you think it would be doing a favor for your brother-in-law to take the place off his hands."

"I'm not really excited about buying any house," he reminded her.

"You should be. Buying a house isn't like buying a pair of shoes. You're talking about a home. A private retreat for you and for the family you might have someday. It's a long-term investment and commitment and it should be important to you. Or you might as well just rent."

Maybe she was afraid she'd revealed a little too much about herself in that lecture—as perhaps she had, he mused. Before he could respond, she had her door open and was standing impatiently in the parking lot.

"The location of this one isn't ideal," she said, her tone emotionless now. "A lot of traffic between here and the hospital at rush hour."

"I don't usually keep a typical rush-hour schedule," he commented lightly, locking the car behind them when he joined her. "But you're right, this wouldn't be my first-choice site."

"We should look at it anyway. Maybe there will be other assets that will outweigh the location."

"Of course." He followed her obediently to the rental office.

Jacqui didn't have to tell him her opinion of that first apartment. He had no trouble at all reading her expression as she wandered through the boxy, sterile, white-painted rooms.

"You might as well live in the O.R.," she said as they climbed back into his car after a very short tour.

"I pretty much do," he replied with a laugh and a shrug.

She snapped her seat belt into place. "But there's no need for you to come home to the same environment. You should feel welcomed and comfortable when you walk into your house, not as though you're still at work."

Fastened into the driver's seat, he started the engine. "Is that the way you feel when you go home to your apartment? Welcomed and comfortable?"

The brief pause that followed his question was heavy, but when she spoke, her tone was even. "No," she admitted. "But that's what I'll look for when I finally buy a place of my own."

He wondered if she'd ever had a home where she had

felt safe and welcome. From what little she'd said of her background, he somehow doubted it. Was that why she'd made a profession of taking care of other peoples' homes?

The next stop was another apartment, this one somewhat nicer and in a beautifully landscaped gated complex. Jacqui gave that one higher marks, both for location and decor. He couldn't say she looked enthusiastic, he thought as they drove away, putting a "maybe" checkmark by that place on the list. But then it was just an apartment. He could be comfortable there, so he'd definitely keep it in mind.

They toured one more apartment and a condo before stopping for lunch. As he had promised, Mitch treated Jacqui to a very nice meal at a popular bistro that specialized in the type of healthy foods she preferred. She seemed to enjoy the meal, but she kept their conversation strictly business, discussing pros and cons of the places they had toured thus far and the advantages and disadvantages of buying versus renting.

Maybe he would have liked to talk about other things during the meal, but he kept reminding himself this wasn't a date. He'd asked her to help him find a place to live, and she was focused intently on doing just that. He wondered what she would say if he told her he was actually enjoying this mission that he'd dreaded all week, mostly because he was having a good time watching her reactions to the places they visited.

He supposed it was only natural that the rental and sales agents they had met assumed they were a couple. Jacqui didn't bother to correct anyone's misconceptions, but he saw her tense a little each time it happened. Maybe it was best if he kept his pleasure in her company to himself. At least for the remainder of this outing.

He'd reserved the three houses on his list for afternoon visits. The first was a big, French-themed house in an exclusive gated neighborhood off Chenal Boulevard in west Little Rock near a golf course and country club. Only two years old, the house had been built to impress, with soaring windows and doorways, impeccable landscaping, top-of-the-line kitchen appliances and decadently luxurious bathrooms. It was all very nice, but he couldn't see himself coming home to this place any more than he could the sterile apartment they'd first toured that morning.

"Honestly?" he said to Jacqui as they drove away, "I prefer Seth's house to that one."

"So do I," she agreed.

Although not as visually impressive as the house they had just seen, Seth's previous home was still a very nice place. It was a safe, clean, quiet neighborhood and Mitch figured he would be comfortable there. He just wasn't sure he wanted to invest in a house when there was always a chance he could decide to take a new position somewhere—maybe as soon as next year, he thought with that familiar ripple of restlessness. Seth's house was a prime example. Seth had bought that house only weeks before meeting Meagan and had lived in it just less than a year before they had married and decided Meagan's house was more suited to the family's needs. Now Seth had to try to find a buyer. Even as nice a place as that one took a while to unload these days.

The second house was a Colonial style, also in west Little Rock but in a more established neighborhood. Mitch liked it well enough, but he couldn't say he liked it more than Seth's house. He could tell Jacqui preferred it to the larger house. She studied all the rooms and poked around in the closets and cupboards. He could almost see her mentally arranging furniture and decorating.

"Nice place," she said about that one afterward.

"It was," he agreed. "But I'm leaning toward the second apartment we saw this morning. Good location. Nice, big rooms. Plenty of parking and storage—not that I have anything to store at the moment. Have to sign a year lease, but that shouldn't be a problem. If I should break the lease for any reason, I'd only have to sacrifice a month's rent."

She murmured something he didn't catch, but there wasn't time to ask her to repeat it. They had arrived at the final house he had scheduled to tour that afternoon.

He thought he heard a muffled sound from Jacqui when he parked in front of the Craftsman-style house in one of Little Rock's oldest, still-well-respected neighborhoods. According to his information, this house had been built in the 1920s. It had been renovated several times since but still retained the flavor of that period, as did most of the houses in the historic area.

Although significantly older and slightly smaller than either of the other houses he'd toured, this one was just as expensive, at the top of his price range. He could see why. All the houses on this block were immaculately maintained, the lawns landscaped and manicured. A curving driveway ended in a discreetly placed garage that matched the house. A roomy front porch was furnished with inviting rockers beneath a lazily turning, antique-style ceiling fan. Flowers bloomed in beds around the porch, and a fountain added the sound of tumbling water to the already idyllic setting.

The inside of the house had been just as skillfully staged. Soft lighting from antique lamps and fixtures cast a welcoming glow over the Mission-styled furnishings arranged for comfort and conversation. Because it was July and still hotter than Hades outside, no fire burned in the old site-built brick fireplace, but it wasn't hard to imagine flames crackling there on a dark winter evening. Built-in shelves held old books and pottery, and antique rugs softened the gleaming wood floors.

The kitchen, though still retaining the flavor of the period, had been renovated into a chef's dream. A sunroom opened off the back, overlooking the small but appealing backyard. They toured a laundry room, a study and a dining room downstairs, then climbed the wooden steps to explore the three bedrooms upstairs. Two smaller bedrooms were separated by a Jack-and-Jill bath, and the master bedroom included a sitting area in a bay window, a bathroom that was as charming as it was luxurious, and not one but two walk-in closets. Because roomy closets hadn't been a feature of this style home at the time it was built, Mitch suspected some walls had been removed to create the space, but the construction had been seamless. It all blended very well.

As many amenities as this house offered, it was more warm and homey to him than the newer places they'd toured earlier. Maybe it was the age, maybe the abundance of honey-toned wood in contrast to the white-painted trim of the other two houses or maybe he just preferred this style. Whatever the reason, he liked it better.

Jacqui, he noted, had very little to say about this one. She'd kept up a running commentary at all the other places and it hadn't been hard to interpret her reactions to them. She studied this house just as closely, if not more so, than the others, but she kept her observations to herself for the most part. She spent an especially long time in the kitchen, gazing at the glass-fronted cabinets, wood-paneled appliances, dark granite countertops and amber-glass light fixtures. If he'd had to guess, he would have said she was transfixed, but it was hard to tell when she made a deliberate effort to mask her thoughts.

She was just stepping out of one of the walk-in closets when he started to enter. Had he not reached up instinctively to grab her shoulders, they would have collided in the doorway. Startled, she laughed. "Oops."

He grinned down at her. "Careful. Even as big as this closet is, there's not room for both of us to get through the doorway at once."

"Then you should move aside so I can come out," she advised him humorously.

He found himself reluctant to release her. It felt good to have his hands on her, to be standing so close he could see the little specks of amber in her dark brown eyes and just a hint of freckles across her lightly tanned nose.

Her smile faded. "Um, Mitch?"

"Yeah." He dropped his hands and moved out of her way. She didn't glance back at him as she wandered off to explore the master bath.

He noted that she looked over her shoulder when he drove away a short while later, her gaze on that house until he'd turned onto busy Kavanaugh Avenue and she could no longer see it. Only then did she turn forward again, adjusting her seat belt and looking through the windshield with a pensive expression.

"That was the last one today," he said, breaking the silence between them when he stopped at a red light. "I don't think my brain can process any more choices."

She smiled faintly, though she didn't turn to look

at him. "I'd say you looked at a nice range of options today."

"Yeah. I can tell my mom I saw apartments, condos and houses, so she can't say I'm not taking the search seriously."

She looked at him then, their eyes meeting for a moment before he directed his attention back to the road ahead. "You're looking at houses to please your mom?"

"I'm looking at houses because I need to move out of my sister's guest room."

"But none of the houses you've seen today have excited you. Not even that last one?"

"It's a house," he answered simply, though he didn't miss her emphasis on the last place they'd seen. She really had liked that one, apparently. "A nice house but still just a place to sleep and stash the stuff I'll eventually reaccumulate."

"You shouldn't rush into anything. Maybe you should wait until some place does excite you."

"Honestly? I don't think that's going to happen. I mean, nothing will really change except my mailing address. I'll still go to work every day at the hospital, still be on call for my mom when she needs me, still hang with my friends when I get the time. A house would add some responsibilities like maintenance and lawn care, but I'd probably have to pay someone to do that stuff most of the time. Mowing and weeding isn't my idea of a good time when I'm off work."

"I wouldn't mind taking care of my own yard, if I had one," she murmured. "Maybe tending some flower beds. But I guess that's not your thing."

He remembered how long she'd gazed at the tidy flower beds around the last house. "No," he replied with a light shrug. "Gardening isn't really something I've had a strong urge to do."

"You want to get away from Little Rock, don't you?"

The seemingly disconnected question caught him off guard, so he hesitated a bit before answering, "I think I've mentioned before that I wouldn't mind seeing what it's like to live somewhere else, because I never have. Every time I thought about moving away for a while, something came up with the family and I felt as though I needed to stay."

"So, what's keeping you now? Your family's in good shape. Your surgical skills are probably in demand just about anywhere you want to move to. Or are you still playing George Bailey?"

Mitch frowned. Was her tone just a little cross? And if so, why? "George who?"

"George Bailey. *It's a Wonderful Life*. The movie."

"Ah." He remembered now. "The guy who kept trying to leave home and couldn't because of the family banking business?"

"Yes."

He chuckled. "I'm no George Bailey. I haven't tried all that hard to leave yet. And, like you said, there's no reason I couldn't move now if I want. I mean, I like my job here, and my family and friends are all here, but still, I can see the appeal of checking out new places. Maybe I'll just find a good home base here and travel when I get the chance—like my upcoming trip to Peru."

"You're really looking forward to that, aren't you?"

"I really am."

"Then I hope the trip will be everything you want it to be."

"Thank you."

As he turned into the driveway of his sister's house,

he glanced across the street toward the for-sale sign in the yard of Seth's former house. He knew it would make his mom happy if he bought that place. Not to mention he'd be doing his brother-in-law a favor. It wasn't as if he didn't get along well enough with the family to live that close. It just didn't— Well, it didn't excite him, he thought, recalling Jacqui's words.

As he followed Jacqui into the house, it occurred to him that the only time that day he'd been anywhere close to excited was when he'd stood in that closet with Jacqui's slender shoulders beneath his hands, her face very close to his.

Something told him that wasn't the type of excitement she had urged him to pursue.

Awakening with a start, Jacqui rolled over to look at the illuminated clock on her bedside. 3:00 a.m. Great.

Knowing she wouldn't sleep again with the echo of her sister's voice in her head, she climbed out of the bed. The house was silent, and she figured Mitch was sound asleep, but she still thought it best not to go traipsing around in nothing but a thigh-length nightshirt—even though he had seen her in that outfit before, she remembered with a slight wince. She pulled on the jeans she'd left draped over the foot of the bed. Figuring that counted as at least mostly dressed, she walked barefoot out of the room, making her way silently down the stairs to the kitchen.

She opened the refrigerator door and reached for a bottle of water. A half bottle of wine caught her eye, but she left it sitting there. That was her mother's sleepless-night crutch, not hers.

Too restless to sit, she leaned against the counter to sip her water. She stared at the table across the shadowy room, but what she saw instead was the kitchen of the Craftsman house she and Mitch had toured that afternoon. She had taken one look at that house and fallen in love. Every step she'd taken inside had only fanned the flames of that passion. The house had been perfect. Exactly the style she and Olivia had always talked about when they'd lay awake at night in a cheap apartment or motel and fantasized about the home they would have someday.

She wanted a house like that. Oh, not that particular one. As much as she had loved it, it had been well out of her price range for any foreseeable future. But she could find a less expensive little house in a less expensive neighborhood and decorate in a similar style. She could paint and hang wallpaper, and she figured she could learn to grout tile and refinish secondhand furniture.

Maybe it was time for her to start haunting estate sales and garage sales on her days off, collecting a few things for the little house she wanted to buy. She'd been in the habit of not accumulating possessions so it would be easier to move when the time came, but she hoped her next move would be into a little house where she could stay for a nice long while. Her goal had been to own a home by the time she turned thirty, just less than a year away. She saw no reason why she couldn't fulfill that dream.

If she had needed any evidence of how different she and Mitch were, she figured their outing today had done the trick. He had looked at apartments and condos and houses with little enthusiasm, seemingly willing to settle for the first reasonably suitable option. From what she could tell, he'd seen the houses as potential anchors, more long-term commitment and responsibility than he was looking for. For someone who had just spent—what had he said, six years?—living in a rented duplex, he certainly saw himself as the footloose type.

Just her luck that the only man who had made her pulse race in the past busy year was a restless surgeon related to her employer—so many strikes against him that it was almost funny. So why wasn't she smiling?

Her somber thoughts were interrupted by a strange sound from the backyard. Frowning, she looked toward the door. Maybe Waldo had heard her moving around and was trying to get her attention. It hadn't sounded like his usual whine, though. Something was...

The sound came again. Catching her breath, she set her water bottle on the counter with a thump and ran toward the door. It took her only moments to disarm the security system and open the locks. "Waldo?"

She could tell at a glance that the dog was in trouble. The trees silhouetted by the backyard security lighting threw long shadows over the pool, patio and lawn, but there was still enough light for her to see that Waldo had somehow become trapped in the fencing designed to hold the adventuresome dog in the yard. His head jammed between a post and a fence slat, he was unable to move anything except his hind quarters. He pumped his back legs wearily, as though he'd been trying for some time to extricate himself, and he whimpered in pain and frustration.

It took only a couple minutes of trying before she conceded she wouldn't be able to free him herself.

"I'll be right back," she assured him, as if he could understand. "Be still so you don't hurt yourself."

Leaving him whining, she dashed inside the house and up the stairs, skidding to a stop in front of Mitch's closed door. She knocked on it sharply. "Mitch? Mitch!"

"Wha?" she heard him say groggily from inside. Moments later the door opened. Tousled and bleary, wearing only a pair of navy pajama bottoms slung low on his hips, he peered down at her. "Jacqui? What's wrong?"

"It's Waldo. Can you help me, please?"

Without taking time to ask any more questions, he followed her quickly downstairs. He assessed the situation with the dog in one quick glance, then knelt on one side of the trapped pet while she crouched on the other side. "Looks like I'm going to have to get some tools. Where does Seth keep his?"

"In the garage storage room." She stroked a hand down the dog's back, feeling the muscles quivering beneath her palm. "I'll stay here with him."

"Okay, be right back."

It took maybe ten minutes for them to free the dog once Mitch returned with a bag of tools. Jacqui assisted him by holding a flashlight and keeping Waldo calm. She wanted to think she could have handled the situation alone if she'd had to, but she was greatly relieved that Mitch seemed to know exactly what to do.

"Is he okay?" she asked, leaning over Mitch's shoulder.

"Let me get him inside in the light where I can see better." Mitch stood, lifting the sixty-pound Lab mix in his arms as easily as if he were picking up a bag of flour. Still weary from the ordeal, Waldo lay limply against Mitch's chest, the tip of his feathery tail wagging in gratitude.

Jacqui and Mitch were both barefoot, so she wasn't surprised when he stumbled a little and cursed beneath his breath on the way toward the house. He righted himself quickly and kept walking to the open back door.

She placed her own feet carefully as she followed behind him.

Mitch set the dog carefully on the kitchen floor. "I'm no veterinarian, but I don't see any problems," he said a moment later.

"There's blood on his neck," Jacqui said, her fingers laced tightly in front of her. Alice loved this dog so much, she thought with a catch in her throat. And Alice wasn't the only one fond of the silly, accident-prone mutt.

"He scraped himself trying to pull free. It's not deep, no need for stitches. If you'll find me a first aid kit, I'll take care of it."

Grateful for something to do, she hurried to get the kit. There was nothing in this house she couldn't locate if necessary.

By the time she returned to the kitchen only minutes later, Waldo was already regaining his usual spirit. He was on his feet, wiggling and expressing his gratitude to Mitch with eager swipes of his tongue.

Chuckling, Mitch fended off the wet kisses, glancing up wryly at Jacqui when she opened the first aid kit. "I think we can safely say he'll be fine."

She watched as he dabbed antibiotic ointment on Waldo's scrapes. "I'm so glad. I swear that dog has more lives than a cat. If you only knew some of the messes he's gotten himself into."

"I've heard a few of them."

"Do you think he'd be stupid enough to stick his head in that hole again tonight?"

"Absolutely," Mitch answered with a laugh.

She sighed. "Then I guess he'll spend the rest of the night—what little there is of it—in the garage until I can get out in the sunlight tomorrow to check the fence."

Mitch scratched the dog's ears, eliciting a blissful tail wag. "He was just exploring. Found an opening and just had to see what was on the other side, right, Waldo?"

Mitch sounded as though he identified all too well with that sentiment.

Comfortable that Waldo had recovered from his ordeal, Jacqui shooed him into the garage, telling him she'd be back in a minute with his food and water dishes and a blanket on which he could rest for his next misadventure. Closing the door into the garage, she turned back to the kitchen.

Mitch stood by the sink, washing his hands. Jacqui frowned when she saw a smudged trail of blood on the tile floor. "I didn't think Waldo bled that much from that little scrape. Maybe there's another—"

And then she realized exactly where the trail led. "Mitch, you're bleeding!"

He glanced down, frowned, then lifted his right foot so he could see the sole. "Well, yeah, I guess I am."

She reached for the first aid kit again. "Sit down, let me look at it."

"That's not— Okay, sure."

She wasn't certain what caused his sudden change of mind, but she didn't ask. She merely knelt in front of him when he plopped into one of the kitchen chairs. She lifted his bleeding right foot into her hands to examine the cut on his heel. "I don't think it's too deep," she said in relief.

"I think I stepped on one of Waldo's toys when I was carrying him in. That's what I get for going outside without shoes, I guess."

"We both did. Silly dog scared me half to death."

She moved to the sink to retrieve a clean washcloth, which she moistened and then carried back to where he sat. She hesitated a moment before kneeling in front of him again. It had suddenly struck her that it was after 3:00 a.m., they were alone in a mostly darkened house, she wore a nightshirt and jeans and Mitch only a pair of pajama bottoms. The intimacy of that situation made her a bit nervous all of a sudden.

Mitch's bland tone helped when he asked, "Want me to do it?"

"No, that would be too awkward for you." Telling herself to snap out of it, she lowered herself to one knee so she could better see the cut. She cleaned the area, dabbed antibiotic ointment on the small cut much as she'd seen Mitch do with Waldo and sealed it with an adhesive bandage. "That should stay on until the bleeding stops."

"Thank you, doctor," he teased.

Flushing a little, she used the still-damp cloth to swipe up the smudges of blood from the floor, then stood to rinse it out and lay it over the sink. She would toss it in with the laundry tomorrow—um, later today, she corrected herself.

"I'm so sorry I had to get you up at this hour," she said, glancing at Mitch, who still sat in the chair watching her fussing with the washcloth. "I hope you don't have to be at the hospital early."

He looked at the clock over the stove. "I planned to be there by seven."

Just a little less than three hours away, Jacqui thought with a wince. "I'm really sorry. I hope you can get a couple more hours of sleep first."

He shrugged. "Actually, I'm wide awake now. I went to bed earlier than usual last night."

"Still, you couldn't have had much more than five hours sleep."

"Five hours was a luxury during my residency. Believe me, I've gotten by on much less." He stood and stretched. The movement dipped his pajama bottoms even lower on his hips and made muscles ripple in his chest and abdomen.

Jacqui's mouth went dry. Making a hasty grab for the open bottle of water she'd left on the counter earlier, she downed several quick swallows—not that it helped much. "Would you—um—like some coffee?"

"I think I'll take a shower. Why don't you go back to bed and try to get some sleep?"

"I'm not sleepy now, either. I'll put on some coffee. It'll be ready by the time you finish showering."

Dropping his arms to his sides, he studied her face intently. "You didn't get up because you heard Waldo, did you? You were already awake?"

She nodded. "I came down for a drink of water. That's when I heard him whimpering."

"You couldn't sleep?"

She shrugged. "I guess I was thirsty."

"You sure there was nothing else?"

When had he moved closer? Setting the water bottle carefully on the counter, she cleared her throat. "I don't know—bad dream, maybe."

"Want to talk about it?"

Because she couldn't look at his eyes just then, she glanced downward. Probably a mistake, she realized immediately, because she was now looking straight at his bare chest. Which was several inches closer than it had been only moments earlier.

"Um, no, I'm fine now, thank you."

"Jacqui—"

Slowly, she lifted her eyes. The way he was looking at her...

She swallowed hard. "Yes?"

"Do I make you nervous?"

Chapter Seven

Apparently, Jacqui didn't like his question. Her chin lifted proudly and her dark eyes narrowed in what might have been a challenge when she replied flatly, "No. You don't make me nervous."

He shook his head slightly in response to the blatant untruth but didn't take her up on the challenge. "Good. I want you to be comfortable with me."

She backed an inch or so away from him, which brought her right up against the kitchen counter behind her. "Of course I am. Didn't we spend all day together?"

"Yes." And she had seemed relaxed enough as long as they were focused on something else, like touring houses or discussing the merits of each. And when they'd worked together to free Waldo from the fence, she'd seemed completely at ease, though worried about the dog. It was only when the focus had shifted to the two of them, alone in a quiet, darkened house, that suddenly her manner had become stilted and self-conscious.

She half turned away from him. "I'll make the coffee."

He reached out to catch her arm, his touch light, making no effort to hold her if she chose to draw back. She didn't immediately pull away, but he sensed that she was poised to do so immediately. "Jacqui."

She looked up at him with that shuttered expression he had no chance to read. "What?"

"The last thing I want to do is make you uncomfortable in any way," he assured her. "But—well, I just think I should tell you I've really enjoyed spending time with you this past week."

He simply couldn't help but believe the attraction he felt for her was not entirely one-sided. There had been too many instances when he'd almost felt the exchange of sparks between them. He had been sure he'd seen an answering awareness in her dark eyes occasionally when she looked at him.

"I'm glad you've enjoyed your stay here," she responded in her best housekeeper voice.

"Don't do that," he said with a slight frown. "You know full well I'm not speaking as an unexpected houseguest."

"Mitch—"

"As least you call me by name now," he mused, his frown tilting into a half smile. "We're making some progress."

"Progress?" she asked suspiciously.

"Progress toward having dinner together without running errands to justify it. Toward talking about things other than our jobs. Toward getting to know each other on a more personal basis than as acquaintances with mutual connections to my family."

She was shaking her head even before he finished speaking. "It wouldn't work, Mitch. There's no need to even think about starting something that has zero chance of going anywhere. Let's just keep things the way they are between us, okay? Friendly. Casual. Semi-professional."

Semi-professional? He might have been wryly amused by the description if he hadn't been so baffled by a fleeting expression he saw in her eyes. Granted, her emotions were hard to read, but he thought he'd nailed that one. Why would Jacqui panic in response to his blatant hints that he wanted to ask her out?

He dropped his hand immediately from her arm, taking a step backward to give her plenty of room. "Like I said, I don't want to make you uncomfortable. I just thought you realized that I'm attracted to you. That I like spending time with you and would like to continue to do so. But if you're not interested, enough said. I won't mention it again and you won't have to give it another thought."

"It isn't that I don't like you," she assured him quickly, as if worried that maybe she'd hurt his pride or his feelings. "It's just that it's all too awkward."

"Because you work for my sister, you mean?"

"That's certainly part of it."

He cocked an eyebrow. "What's the other part?"

"Well, you know—" Frowning, she drew a sharp breath. "I'm not interested in playing Vivian to your Edward, Mitch."

"I have no idea what that means," he said with a puzzled laugh.

"Pretty Woman."

"Ah. Another movie allusion."

She shrugged. "I spent a lot of time watching movies on fuzzy motel TVs when I was growing up."

He would definitely like to hear more about her past, but this wasn't the time to ask the questions that buzzed in his mind. Instead, he shook his head. "I saw that movie a few years back. Hardly a suitable comparison. Vivian was no housekeeper."

"Okay, fine," she said with an impatient wave of her hand. "Then let's just say I'm not interested in playing the role of Cinderella."

"And I wouldn't have a clue how to play Prince Charming," he replied evenly. "I'm just Mitch. And I'd like to get to know Jacqui better."

"There's not that much to know. I moved around a lot, have a distantly polite relationship with my parents, clean and cook for a living and do a little knitting in my spare time."

That was how she summed up her life? "You forgot to add that you are intelligent and competent—not to mention strikingly attractive. Or that you do more than clean and cook for this family—you keep them on schedule and reassured that their precious daughter is well cared for while they're pursuing their careers. They trust you with their home and her welfare. That says a great deal about your character."

A hint of pink darkened her cheeks. "That's all very nice of you to say, but still…you and I couldn't be more different."

"Oh." He smiled crookedly. "So I'm not smart, attractive or competent?"

She gave him a look of censure. "That's not what I meant."

"I haven't moved around at all, I'm close to my

mother and sisters and I basically do bone carpentry for a living. In my spare time, I play some soccer. Sure, that's a different background than yours, but you still haven't convinced me why you think we're so unsuited. Unless, of course, it comes back to you being completely uninterested in me."

"It's not that exactly—"

Taking encouragement from the murmur, he moved a little closer again. "Or that you find me unattractive."

"Obviously you're a good-looking man. But I—"

"So answer this. If I weren't Meagan's brother, would you go out with me if I asked?"

"If you weren't Meagan's brother, we'd have never met," she pointed out somewhat brusquely. "Surgeons and housekeepers hardly move in the same circles."

"If I repaired cars instead of bones and we'd met, say, at the grocery store in the produce aisle, would you go out with me?"

Her mouth twitched with what might have been a reluctant smile. "That's a lot of ifs."

He shrugged but didn't look away from her face.

"Okay, maybe," she said after a moment. "If all those things were true—which they aren't—I might consider going out with you. But even then, I doubt it would go anywhere. There are other things that would get in the way."

He figured they could work on those other things later. At least they had established that she wasn't entirely indifferent to him. He smiled. "Then let's pretend and see what happens. If it doesn't work out, then there's nothing lost, right?"

"I've never been very good at pretending."

He lifted her chin and brushed a light kiss over the lips he had been wanting to taste for much longer than he'd acknowledged even to himself. The kiss was too fleeting for her to really respond, but he thought he felt her lips move just a little before he drew away.

Stepping back, he grinned. "I'm going to take that shower now. I have a couple of broken cars to check on this morning."

"Mitch—"

He thought it best to just keep walking. She didn't try to detain him again.

Mitch's rounds at the hospital didn't take long. He had no surgeries scheduled for that Sunday morning and wasn't on call, so he just checked on a few patients, consulted with some parents and had a quick meeting with a couple of residents before calling it a day before noon.

"I was just going to grab an early lunch, Mitch. Want to join me?" a friend asked when they met in the hallway.

"Thanks, Dan, but I have plans. Next time, okay?"

"Sure. See you."

Nodding, Mitch walked on toward the elevators. He liked to keep moving when he was on his way out. Stopping to talk was just asking to be detained for one reason or another.

Connor Hayes, a second-year resident in pediatrics, was already on the elevator when Mitch stepped in. Connor had rotated through the surgery unit when Mitch was a resident and Connor still a med student. They were close to the same age. Connor hadn't started medical school until he was thirty, unlike Mitch, who'd entered right after college.

"How's it going, Connor?"

The other man nodded a greeting. "I'm good, thanks.

I heard about the fire, Mitch. Is there anything I can do for you?"

"Thanks, but I've got everything under control. Sort of," he added with a chuckle. "Still have some shopping to do, but I've got enough to get by for a while."

"Were you able to salvage anything?"

Mitch shook his head. "Lost it all."

"I'm sorry to hear that."

"Thanks. How's your family?"

The elevator door opened into the parking garage and Connor fell into step beside Mitch to reply. "All doing well, thanks. Alexis is eleven now, thinks she's grown. Anthony is five months, and growing like a weed. And Mia somehow juggles her work and motherhood and my crazy schedule without blinking an eye, just like always."

Mitch chuckled. "Tell her I said hello, will you?"

"I will, thanks."

Mitch was still thinking about that brief conversation with Connor when he buckled himself into his car a few minutes later. An Arkansas native, Connor had married a local woman, attended college and medical school in the state and had listed the local children's hospital as his first choice when applying for his residency program. He seemed to have no interest whatsoever in leaving the state where he had spent his entire life, settling happily into marriage, fatherhood and the medical career he had worked hard to attain. Granted, Mitch didn't know Connor well, but if Connor felt at all constrained by his deeply rooted lifestyle, Mitch had seen no signs of it.

Mitch loved his job. Was close to his mother and sisters. Had really good friends here. So what was missing in his life that made him yearn for something more? A house, wife, kids? He wanted all those things eventually, of course, but he hadn't really given them much thought until this point. His restlessness had seemed to tug him in other directions—adventures and experiences outside what he had always known here. And now that his rented house was gone, his possessions few, his family all in good health and busy with their own lives, he wasn't sure what was holding him back from actively looking for someplace new to try.

His thoughts turned to Jacqui, who had been in his mind so much lately. She was certainly different from the women he'd dated before. Was that part of his fascination with her? From what he had gathered, her background was almost diametrically opposite to his, enough to seem exotic to him. Was she right to worry that he was only amusing himself with her while he was at loose ends—if that was, indeed, why she was so hesitant about spending more time with him.

He couldn't accept that unrealistic excuse she'd given about not wanting to play Cinderella to his Prince Charming. Seriously, who thought that way these days? He had never paid attention to social class distinctions, and even if he did, it wasn't as if he came from a highbrow background. His dad had been a sci-fi-loving physics professor at a state university, his mom was an accountant—people who worked hard at their jobs to pay the bills and support their families. The fact that all three of their offspring had attended medical school was mostly coincidence—or maybe the younger two had been influenced by the older sibling's choice. Meagan had teasingly claimed they were always copying her.

As far as Mitch was concerned, it was just a job—a good job, sure, one that required a lot of training and paid well afterward, but still simply the career he had chosen. Jacqui ran his sister's household, which required skills plenty of people lacked. He couldn't see why their choice of vocations should have anything to do with their being friends. Maybe more than friends.

But if Jacqui was fretting about that foolish quibble, then it looked as though it was up to him to convince her differently. There might be other reasons why a flirtation—or more—between them wouldn't work, but he wasn't going to let anything as superficial as tax brackets keep them from finding out for sure. Not if he could help it anyway.

One thing about Mitch Baker, the guy was certainly persuasive. Jacqui wasn't sure how he'd talked her into an outing Sunday evening, but she found herself sitting beside him in a movie theater, sharing a tub of popcorn and watching an action film play on the giant screen. Maybe she'd accepted because it was less awkward being out in public with him than alone in the house. It was hard to be tense and formal with popcorn grease on their fingers and oversize 3-D glasses perched on their noses.

Watching Mitch laughing at a groan-worthy pun from one of the main characters, tossing popcorn kernels in his mouth and peering through the plastic lenses, it was hard to imagine him in an operating room, gowned and gloved and barking orders while piecing together a child's shattered bones. She pushed that image out of her mind immediately. This Mitch, the one in jeans and silly glasses, was someone with whom she could relax, have fun, flirt a little. The other Mitch—well, she didn't even know him.

It wasn't that she didn't think herself good enough to date a doctor, she assured herself. As battered as it had been, her self-esteem wasn't quite that low. The problem was that she didn't have enough in common with that other Mitch—the one with advanced degrees and enough money to look at houses in some of the nicest neighborhoods. The Mitch who could look at those houses and feel no excitement at the thought of owning one and nesting contentedly into it.

He laughed again at an on-screen antic and grinned at her to share the joke. He looked so cute and silly in the big glasses that she had to smile back. There was no reason she couldn't enjoy spending a few hours with this Mitch. It wasn't as if she'd had all that many dates lately—not that this was a date, exactly, she corrected herself quickly. Still, she figured it was good for her to keep her socializing skills from getting too rusty.

She reached for another handful of popcorn.

Of course, every date had to end. In her experience, they most often ended at the door. It was awkward enough dealing with the good-night kiss decision after an ordinary first date. It felt even more strange having Mitch follow her inside, knowing they would be sharing breakfast—and not because she had invited him to stay.

Not that this evening had been a real date, of course.

"How about some tea?" Mitch asked when they walked inside the house. "You like to drink tea at night, right?"

"Yes, I do," she agreed. "I'll make some."

"I'll do it," he corrected her. "I think it's my turn to make the tea. I've watched you use that fancy boiling-water dispenser at the sink, and I know where you store the teas, so I can manage."

A little flustered by the offer, she stammered, "I, uh—"

"Chamomile, right?"

"Yes, but—"

"It'll be ready in just a few minutes."

She blinked after him as he headed for the kitchen. Her kitchen, she thought with a slight frown. Well, not really, but there was no denying she was a bit proprietary about it. She heard a muted crash from that direction and she winced. She'd fed Waldo before leaving that evening, but she supposed it wouldn't hurt to wander casually through the kitchen to check on him—and a few other things.

She forced herself to remain in the living room instead. To give her hands something to do, she pulled out her knitting. She was working on a new pattern, a pretty lacework shawl with a delicate scalloped edge. She'd chosen a fine, shell-pink yarn, and the project was turning out nicer than she had even expected. She usually made heavier scarves and shawls, fashioned more for warmth and comfort than delicacy.

Mitch returned to the room with a steaming cup of tea in each hand, a frown of concentration on his face as he made an effort not to spill them. "That's a pretty thing you're making. What is it?"

She set the project aside to reach for her tea. "A shawl."

"Something you're going to sell in your friend's shop?"

"I haven't decided yet. It could be a gift for someone."

He sat at the other end of the sofa and they chatted about the movie while they sipped their tea. When they'd run out of things to say about the lightweight plot, they fell silent. Jacqui couldn't think of a thing to say to fill the suddenly noticeable quiet. The comfort she had felt with Mitch at the theater was dissipating now, leaving her inexplicably ill at ease again and much too aware of him sitting next to her.

She drained the tea in a long swallow, almost burning her throat because it was still hot. Fortunately, she managed not to sputter. That would have been embarrassing, she thought with a slight wince. "I'm getting really tired. Not much sleep last night. I think I'll go check on Waldo and then head up to bed."

Studying her face, Mitch nodded. "Sounds like a plan. I'll just watch the news and then I'll probably turn in."

Looking as though he'd settled where he was for a while, he reached for the television remote control as she stood with her empty teacup. He didn't act at all as though they'd just been out on a date. So maybe she wasn't the only one who had chosen not to view it in that light.

And how foolish was it that her feminine ego was just a little piqued that his attention had already wandered away from her to the TV?

"Thanks for taking me to the movie," she said, hovering in the doorway. "I had a very nice time."

He glanced away from the screen to send her a smile. "Thank you for going with me. I've been wanting to see that film."

"Sure. So, um, good night. then."

"Good night. I'll be leaving very early in the morning, so don't bother trying to get up to make breakfast. I'll grab something at the hospital."

She nodded, hesitated another microsecond, then turned to carry her teacup to the kitchen. For some reason, she felt as though there was something more she should have said, but she couldn't for the life of her decide what it might have been. Mitch was already watching TV again anyway.

Maybe he hadn't found her as interesting as he'd thought he would once he'd actually talked her into sort of going out with him. So much for her concerns about whether there would come an awkward attempt at a good-night kiss.

Realizing she was pouting a little, she pulled her bottom lip firmly back into place and told herself she was glad that precarious experiment was behind them now.

Mitch waited until Jacqui was out of his sight before releasing a long, pent-up breath. If she'd had any idea how hard it had been for him not to at least try to kiss her tonight, she'd probably have bolted from the room. Her lips had been so tempting when she'd pursed them slightly to blow on her hot tea, when she'd lowered her cup to leave her mouth moist and glistening. But he had been determined to prove to her that she didn't have to worry about staying alone in this house with him even though he'd told her earlier that he was attracted to her.

He had no intention of taking advantage of their situation. Of putting her in an awkward situation with her employer's brother. The fact that they were both staying here was unrelated to what he hoped was a developing connection between them, other than the fact that the enforced proximity had made him realize just how strong his attraction to her had always been.

Now, if only he didn't do anything to run her off—figuratively, at least—before he even had a chance to see where that attraction could lead.

* * *

Jacqui could tell when Mitch dragged in at 9:00 p.m. Monday that he'd had a rough day. She'd gotten a call four hours earlier from his pleasant and efficient secretary informing her that Dr. Baker was in surgery and would not be home in time for dinner. Though she'd been a bit surprised by the call, Jacqui had thanked the woman for the call, and she'd been touched that Mitch had gone to the effort of getting the message to her.

She wouldn't have minded if he'd simply not shown up for dinner, of course. He certainly had no obligation to eat there every evening, whether he notified her or not. From experience with her employers' somewhat erratic schedules, she cooked nothing that couldn't be safely stowed in the fridge and reheated later. But it had been thoughtful of him to let her know.

Taking one look at his face when he walked into the living room, she set her knitting aside and jumped to her feet. "You look worn out. Have you had anything to eat?"

"I'm not hungry, thanks."

It wasn't exactly an answer about when he'd last eaten, but she didn't bother arguing with him. Even at this hour, it was still hot as blazes outside on this first Monday in August, so she didn't offer hot tea. Instead, she said, "Sit down. I'll get you something cold to drink. There's fresh lemonade or a pitcher of iced tea. Which would you prefer?"

"You don't have to—"

"Mitch," she broke in firmly. "Which do you want?"

"Tea, please," he conceded, sinking onto the couch.

"I'll be right back."

He had his head back when she returned only moments later, carrying a glass of tea and a plate of cheese, crackers, carrot sticks and olives, with a couple of cookies on the side—just in case he decided he was a little hungry after all.

"Thanks." Accepting the glass, he smiled wryly when she set the food in front of him, but after taking only a couple of sips of the tea, he stacked cheese on a cracker and popped it into his mouth.

She sat on the other end of the couch, ready to hop up and run for more food if he still looked hungry after finishing this light snack. "Rough day, huh?"

He shrugged. "Tougher than most. Had an emergency come in just as I was getting ready to leave for the day. Eight-year-old boy, both legs shattered in an ATV accident. He was too young to be riding the four-wheeler at all, of course, but at least he was wearing a helmet, which probably saved his life. We were in the O.R. for three hours. And that was after an already long day of procedures, one of which had complications that made it take longer than it should have."

"So you've been on your feet all day?"

Crunching a carrot stick, he nodded. "I'm usually on my feet," he said after swallowing. "This was just a longer day than most."

"Let me get you some more tea." She jumped up to fetch the pitcher because he seemed to be very thirsty. He'd already almost drained his glass.

Pushing the empty plate aside a few minutes later, he leaned back against the cushions again with a light sigh. "That was good. Thanks."

"Can I get you anything else?"

"No, really. I had plenty, thank you."

She turned on the couch to look at him. "The little boy who was hurt? Will he be okay?"

"He has a long recuperation ahead of him, but he'll get there. Kids are pretty resilient."

Not always, she thought with a ripple of sadness she didn't want him to see.

But Mitch seemed to be getting better at reading her. He must have followed the direction her thoughts had taken. "Jacqui?" he asked after a pause. "Do you mind if I ask how you lost your sister?"

She felt her chest tighten but answered evenly. "In a car accident twelve years ago. The surgeons worked very hard to save her, but she died on the table."

"Younger or older sister?"

"Younger."

"I'm very sorry."

She nodded. "It's difficult for me to talk about it."

"I won't press you, then. Just know that if you ever need to talk, I'm a good listener."

"Thank you."

Sipping the last of his second glass of tea, he reached up with his free hand to squeeze the back of his neck. The gesture seemed to be automatic, as if he were hardly aware that he was even doing it.

Her awareness of the reason for his discomfort—a long operation on an injured eight-year-old boy—overcame her hesitation. "If your neck is stiff, I'd be happy to give you a quick massage. I've been told I'm pretty good at it."

He dropped his hand, looking first surprised then intrigued by her offer. "My neck is a little sore."

Because he was so much taller, she moved to stand behind him as he leaned back against the couch cushions. The back of the couch was low enough that she had full access to his neck and shoulders, especially when he lowered his chin a little. Focusing strictly on finding and alleviating the knots in his muscles, she tried without much success to ignore the warmth and strength of him beneath her palms, even through his thin-knit shirt. When she worked on his nape, his thick hair tickled her fingers, tempting her to bury her hands in it.

A particularly stubborn knot just above his right shoulder blade required both her thumbs to work out. His low groan of pained pleasure signified the massage was working. The deep rumble vibrated through her, stirring something deep inside her. Her fingers tightened for a moment, causing him to flinch just a little. Murmuring an apology, she lightened her touch, carefully working the knotted muscle into relaxation.

After another few moments, she rested her hands on his shoulders. "Better?"

He reached up to lay his hands over hers, holding her in position. "Much better. Thank you."

"You're welcome."

Twisting his neck, he smiled up at her, still holding her hands. "You were told correctly, by the way. You are very good at that."

"Um, thanks." She was held captive as much by his gaze as by his hands on hers. She found herself unable to look away from the expression in his darkening blue eyes.

His smile faded. "Jacqui."

She would never know what impulse took hold of her then. Whatever it was, she leaned over before she could talk herself out of it and gave in to an urge she'd been trying to resist for the past ten minutes—oh, heck, for the past ten days.

She pressed her lips firmly against his.

Chapter Eight

Mitch was certainly quick. One minute she was standing behind the couch, leaning over to kiss him, the next she found herself tumbled into his lap, his arms around her, his lips moving avidly against hers. It was as if he'd just been biding his time until she made the first move and had been poised for an immediate response.

That fleeting brush of lips the night before had been merely a hint of what was to come, whetting her appetite and stirring her imagination. But this...this was so much more than she had even anticipated. There was no first-kiss awkwardness, no bumping of noses or fumbling of hands. He kissed her as though they had known each other—intimately—forever, his mouth fitting itself perfectly to hers, his tongue greeting hers as if he already knew exactly how she would taste and feel, his hands settling exactly in the right places to give her the maximum pleasure from his touch without making her uncomfortable by going too far.

"Do you know how long I've wanted to do that?" he asked when he finally gave them both a chance to breathe.

She rested her hand lightly against his face, feeling the slight roughness of his late-evening beard, the firm line of his jaw. "Since you fell over my suitcase and I tried to attack you with a candlestick?"

He chuckled. "No—though I won't deny I wanted to kiss you then. The first time I met you I had stopped by Seth's house to give something to Meagan, back when she and Seth were dating and Seth and Alice still lived across the street. You walked into the room carrying a big vase of fresh flowers to set on the table in the foyer, and I remember thinking you were even prettier than the roses in your hands."

She blinked in surprise, clearly recalling the moment he referred to. Meagan had introduced them. "Jacqui, this is my brother, Mitch," Meagan had said casually.

Jacqui's first jolt of attraction toward the nice-looking man smiling at her had been firmly shoved aside when she'd remembered that Meagan's brother was also a surgeon. She had nodded pleasantly, then asked him in her housekeeper voice if she could take his coat and get him anything to drink. When he'd politely declined the drink, she'd made an excuse about work to do and disappeared for the remainder of his visit with his sister. The awareness she had felt for him that first time had never completely gone away, try as she might to convince herself otherwise when she had seen him since.

She was startled that he, too, still remembered so clearly the first time they met.

"I've been wanting to get to know you better ever since," he added, studying her face for her reaction.

"That was almost a year ago. You never gave any indication that you were…well, interested in me."

He shrugged, settling her more comfortably against him. "It was awkward."

She bit her lip for a moment before murmuring, "It's still awkward."

"It doesn't have to be. We're both single, unattached adults. There's no reason at all we can't spend time together when we want."

She could already feel some of her earlier misgivings building inside her again. "And when it ends? I'll still work for your sister, and because of that, our paths will continue to cross occasionally. Can we just go on the way we have been, pretending nothing changed?"

He gave a little laugh and brushed a strand of her tousled, short hair from her temple. "We're just starting to talk about this and already you're worrying about a theoretical ending at some possible point in the future?"

She grimaced. "I can't help it. I like to know what to expect from my future. Where I'll be, what I'll be doing. As much as possible, I try to anticipate all the possible outcomes of any major decisions I make."

His left arm propped on the couch behind her, he continued to toy with the ends of her hair with his right hand when he asked lightly, "Does that need to control the future come from your childhood?"

She still wasn't really ready to discuss her past with him, but she answered candidly. "Probably. I never knew from one week to the next where I'd be living or going to school. All I ever wanted was to settle down in one place and make a home for myself there."

His fleeting frown made her wonder if her admission worried him a little. He'd made no secret of his own restlessness—a result of a childhood that was too settled and predictable, in his view.

Maybe opposites attracted, but there had to be more than attraction to form a lasting bond. But then, Mitch wasn't worried about forming lasting bonds, she reminded herself, studying his face through her lashes. Maybe he was concerned that she was looking for more from him than he had been prepared to offer. Her talk about permanence and settling down could have made him nervous.

She smiled slightly and shook her head. "Like you said, all we've done is share a few kisses. Satisfying our curiosity, I suppose. I'm not worrying about the future tonight."

"That's what you think we're doing? Satisfying curiosity?"

"I suppose so. I have to confess I've wondered what it would be like to kiss you," she said with a smile, trying to downplay her action in initiating that first kiss.

His mouth twitched. "Yeah? So how was it?"

Relieved that he seemed to be following her lead in keeping this light, she said after a moment of feigned deliberation, "It was nice."

His eyebrows rose. "Nice? That's the best you can say?"

She couldn't help but laugh at his tone. "Okay, *very* nice."

Wrapping his left arm around her, he nestled her closer. "I'd like to try for a more enthusiastic endorsement."

She barely hesitated before lifting her mouth to his. Okay, so this wasn't going anywhere. There was no need to try to control the future because there was no future for her and Mitch beyond tonight. Alice would be home tomorrow, so this was the last night she and Mitch would be alone in the house. Whatever happened between them tonight, it ended at daylight.

It certainly wouldn't be the first time she'd metaphorically folded her tents and moved on. She knew how to put the past behind her, how to lock memories away to be savored or suffered in private. She might as well enjoy what she had started.

"Well?" His voice was husky when he finally drew back a few inches, a warm flush of color on his cheeks, a glint of heat in his eyes. As close as she was to him, she knew exactly how aroused he was by the long kisses they had shared. Just as he could probably read similar signs from her.

"Much better than nice," she assured him, her own voice breathy.

He rested his forehead against hers, releasing a long, slow sigh. He stroked his right hand slowly up and down her left arm, his touch both soothing and further arousing. "I'd better go on up to bed. Thanks for the neck rub. And…everything else."

She blinked rapidly, trying to process what he'd just said. "You're, um, going to bed?"

Alone? Not that she necessarily would have agreed to go with him if he'd asked, but—wasn't he going to ask?

Drawing away from her, he gave her a crooked smile. "Yes. I told you, Jacqui, I won't take advantage of our situation. Our sharing this house because of outside circumstances, I mean. It would be different if we were at your place, and you'd invited me in and one thing led to another…" He let the words drift off into a rueful shrug.

So that was why he had focused so fiercely on the TV

the night before, sending her off to bed after their movie date with hardly a second look. Why he was drawing back tonight after kissing her until her willpower was decidedly weakened. He was being chivalrous. The jerk.

"I'm quite capable of making decisions for myself without being influenced by 'outside circumstances,'" she said coolly. "If I choose not to be taken advantage of, trust me, there would be no advantage taken."

He looked as though he might have laughed at her wording but was making an effort not to. Wise choice.

Catching his shirt in both hands, she pulled him into another hard kiss. She had started this tonight. She would call an end to it. Eventually.

The buzz of a cell phone broke them apart, winded and dazed and startled by the interruption. Mitch reached automatically for the phone on his belt, then stopped himself when they realized it was Jacqui's rarely used, but always at hand, phone demanding attention.

Glancing at the screen, she frowned. She wouldn't have been overly surprised had she seen Alice's number displayed there, but it made her nervous to realize that it was Alice's grandmother calling. "Hello?"

"Jacqui, it's Paulette Burns," the older woman said, confirming the caller ID. "Have you, um, heard from Alice?"

Jacqui felt herself go cold. "No. Why? What's wrong?"

Mitch stirred beside her, probably picking up on her misgivings.

"She went to the lake with her friends for a picnic and a swim, followed by ice cream in town. They said they'd be back by nine but it's ten now and we haven't heard from her. We've tried calling her cell, but she's not answering. Of course, there are several places up here where it's hard to get service, so she could be in one of those spots."

Jacqui drew a very deep breath and counseled herself to speak calmly despite her rising distress. "What friends is she with, Mrs. Burns? She didn't mention this plan to me."

After a pause, Alice's grandmother said, "She implied that you knew about it. It's a few of her friends from there in Little Rock. Swim team friends, she said, so we didn't worry about them swimming at the dam site. I believe there were four of them going, counting Alice. We told her to be careful and to be home by nine so she wouldn't be out after dark. Harold's thinking maybe he should drive around to see if he can find them."

Jacqui moistened her suddenly dry lips. "Who's driving Alice, Mrs. Burns? One of the mothers?"

"No, it's that young man. Her uncle's friend. He seemed quite nice and responsible. Michael?"

Jacqui looked at Mitch, who was watching her intently. "Do you mean Milo?"

"Yes, that's it. Milo."

"I'll kill him," Mitch muttered with a scowl.

"I'll try to call her, and then I'll call you right back," Jacqui said into her phone. She needed a moment to collect herself, to think about what the next step should be. Call the police? Jump in her car and make the forty-five-minute drive to Heber Springs to look for Alice herself? "Give me five minutes."

"All right. I'm sorry to worry you, but we weren't exactly sure what to do. Alice has never done anything like this with us before."

"What's going on?" Mitch asked when Jacqui lowered

her phone. Both of them were on their feet now, and he didn't take his eyes off her face, which she knew must be drained of color.

Hearing the slight unsteadiness in her own voice, she gave him a quick summary of Alice's escapade. "She led her grandparents to believe I knew about the plan," she added grimly. "When I find her…"

He rested a hand on her shoulder when her words faded into a taut silence. "I'm sure she's fine." He sounded as though he was trying to reassure himself as much as her. "Someone would have called if anything had happened. She's probably having fun and lost track of time."

"I told her I didn't want her riding in a car with teenagers. She knew I wouldn't have approved this plan. How could her grandparents have let her go with them? They're supposed to be watching her!"

"Maybe they've forgotten how to control a teenager. And Alice has never pulled a stunt like this before that I know of, so she must have caught them off guard."

Jacqui nodded tightly. "That's what Mrs. Burns said."

"Okay, first thing we need to do is find Alice. We can call…"

Jacqui jumped when the phone buzzed and vibrated in her hand. A glance at the screen made her close her eyes momentarily in relief before she spoke. "Alice?"

"I'm sorry, Jacqui."

The miserable tone in the girl's voice didn't soften Jacqui's own one bit. "Where are you?"

"I just got back to my grandparents' house. I didn't know it was so late."

"You've forgotten how to tell time?"

Jacqui could almost hear the girl wince in response

to the sharp tone of the question. "I guess I didn't look at the clock," Alice muttered. "I'm sorry."

"First, you should be apologizing to your grandparents for worrying them. And for misleading them that this harebrained idea had been approved ahead of time. You and I will be having a long talk tomorrow. And I have a feeling your father will be discussing this with you when he gets home later this week. I wouldn't be surprised if your mother hears about it when she talks to her parents. She'll probably have a few things to say to you, also."

"You're going to tell Dad?" Alice wailed. That was the warning out of Jacqui's litany that seemed to concern her most—and rightly so. Jacqui had only seen Seth mad once or twice in the time she had known him, and she would hate to be on the wrong end of that cool, lawyer-sharp temper.

Alice wouldn't be pulling a stunt like this again any time in the near future, Jacqui predicted.

"I'll see you tomorrow," she said. "In the meantime, you be extremely polite and considerate to your grandparents so your visit with them doesn't end entirely badly."

"I will. I guess you're pretty mad, huh?"

"You could say that. Are your friends on their way home? Have they called their parents to let them know they're safe?"

"It was just Maggie and Kelly and Milo. Kelly's parents are out of town. She's spending a couple of nights with Maggie. Maggie told her mom they were coming up to visit me at my grandparents' house at the lake and that a friend of my uncle's was driving—and that's true," she added with a just a hint of renewed defiance. "They just called Maggie's mom and said they were on their way home. Maggie doesn't have to be supervised all the time like I do."

Maggie, who Jacqui knew through Alice's swim team, was a year older than Alice and the daughter of a single mother who had never seemed focused enough on parenting in Jacqui's opinion. Alice had been invited to several unchaperoned parties at Maggie's house, which Seth and Meagan had refused to allow her to attend. Jacqui would have done the same, had it been up to her to make the decision. From now on, Jacqui would be keeping a closer eye on Alice's association with Maggie—as she suspected Seth and Meagan would be.

After a few more terse words with Alice, Jacqui disconnected the call with a low groan. "I will be so glad when Seth and Meagan get back in town," she said on a hearty exhale. "They're the ones who should be dealing with Alice's sudden teenage insanity, not me."

"She's okay?"

"Yes."

Mitch visibly relaxed a little when Jacqui repeated what Alice had told her. "I'll have a chat with Milo tomorrow," he promised. "I'll get his number from Scott, who is also going to hear how I feel about his worthless brother hanging around with a group of fourteen- and fifteen-year-old girls. Trust me, after tomorrow, Milo will turn and walk in the other direction whenever he sees Alice."

"She'll be angry with you," Jacqui warned, believing absolutely that Milo would avoid Alice from now on. She'd never seen Mitch look quite this intimidating. And it irked her that she responded quite physically to that look.

Mitch shrugged. "She'll get over it. Or she won't.

Either way, she won't be in a car with Milo Lemon again."

"Good."

Wearily, she pushed a hand through her hair, not caring that the gesture left it in spikes around her face. The mood was broken tonight. She might as well go on up to bed. Alone. Not that she expected to sleep well.

She would be glad when Seth and Meagan returned from their trip and life could get back to normal. Everything had been just fine before they'd left her in charge of their house and their daughter and a stormy summer night had left her sharing this house with Dr. Mitch Baker. Despite what he'd said about being attracted to her from the start, despite his surprisingly clear memory of the first time they had met, despite his insistence that their very different careers had no significance at all to him, she still had no intention of letting herself get carried away by improbable fantasies.

"I'm going up to bed," she said. "Good night, Mitch."

If he was surprised by her abrupt departure, he didn't let it show. "I'll stay down here for a while. Maybe watch the news before I turn in. Good night, Jacqui."

She turned without another word and headed for the stairs. It felt as though more than a long day had just come to an end.

Too restless to sleep, Mitch drank another glass of tea while he watched the ten o'clock local news. When the newscast ended, he carried his glass into the kitchen and placed it in the dishwasher. He supposed he really should turn in; he had another long day scheduled tomorrow. But he was still wired. Both Jacqui and Alice had left him tied up in knots that evening.

Women, he thought with a rueful shake of his head.

There was no way any man could fully understand them—and that gender chasm developed young, judging by his niece's behavior. He chuckled when the thought crossed his mind that Jacqui could be upstairs right now thinking that men were impossible to understand at any age. His amusement faded when it occurred to him that he understood Milo all too well—which was why he'd be having a long talk with that young man very soon.

Glancing toward the back patio door, he saw a nose pressed against the glass, a pair of eyes watching him as he moved around the kitchen. "Hey, Waldo."

He wasn't sure if the dog had heard him, but Waldo knew he had Mitch's attention now. The dog yelped and wagged his tail eagerly.

"Now don't start barking. You'll wake everyone up," Mitch chided, moving quickly to the door.

He stepped outside into the still-stifling August night. It was fully dark now, but sundown had provided little relief from the heat and humidity. The weather forecaster Mitch had just watched had predicted temperatures reaching close to a hundred degrees Fahrenheit by the end of the week. The hospitals would be busy treating heat-related injuries. Having lived here all his life, Mitch was accustomed to hot, dry summers, but he had to admit he preferred the cooler days of spring and fall.

He sat for a while on the patio, patting Waldo, who had recovered nicely from his fence encounter. Surrounding them were the sounds of a Southern summer night as the mostly young professionals in the neighborhood settled in to sleep in preparation for the next workday. The soothing chirps of frogs and crickets in the narrow band of woods at the back of the subdivision blended with the occasional rumble of passing cars on the quiet streets. A siren wailed in the distance, the fading sound coming from the direction of downtown. A dog barked from a neighboring yard, answered by another farther down the block. Waldo cocked his head in response to that brief, canine conversation but didn't join in. He seemed completely happy to sit at Mitch's feet having his head and ears rubbed.

Though the security lighting in the neighborhood dimmed the cloudless night sky, Mitch could just see the glimmer of stars overhead and the blinking lights of a high-passing plane. A nearly full moon floated serenely over the sleepy scene, its reflection glittering on the water of the inground pool that took up about half of the good-size backyard. The pool was surrounded by a decorative, wrought-iron fence. Meagan had laughingly confided that Waldo would play in the pool for hours if they didn't keep it fenced and that the dog enjoyed tossing toys, sticks and anything else he could find into the water they tried to keep clean.

Life in a peaceful Little Rock neighborhood. These were the sounds and sights Mitch had experienced all his life. He had spent a month one summer during high school working on a friend's rural family farm, and although he had enjoyed the experience, he'd learned then that he wasn't really suited to country living. He liked living in the city.

Because it was separated into such distinct neighborhoods, Little Rock was known as a good-size city with a small-town feel. The largest in the state, the capitol city had a population of just less than 700,000. It had its share of urban issues, like any metropolis. Some neighborhoods struggled with poverty, crime and drugs, and he had seen the results of those problems all too often during his training at the teaching hospital. The children's hospital where he worked now had received national acclaim for its excellence, and he was proud to be associated with it. And yet...

He wished he knew for sure whether the restiveness inside him was a result of wanderlust or some other deficiency in his life. Would he be more enthusiastic about settling permanently into a place of his own—like those houses he'd toured the past Saturday—if he had someone special with whom to share that house? A family to fill the empty bedrooms? His own dog in his own backyard?

For some reason, he glanced up toward Jacqui's bedroom window then, seeing no lights shining there. Was she lying awake replaying their kisses in her mind? Did she, too, ache with a hunger to carry those embraces further? Were her nerves still thrumming, her skin still oversensitized, her pulse still erratic—as his were? Or was she sleeping peacefully up there alone, maybe even relieved that they had been interrupted before they'd both gotten carried away by attraction and proximity?

He rose abruptly. "Okay, dog, I'm going to bed. Alice will be home tomorrow, so you'll get plenty of attention then."

Assuming, of course, that Jacqui didn't lock the girl in her room until her father was home again to take over her supervision, he thought, only half-jokingly. He couldn't say he would blame Jacqui for being tempted to do just that.

Locking the kitchen door behind him and resetting the alarm system, he turned out the lights and headed quietly up the stairs. He had to pass Jacqui's door on the way to his room. He paused when he heard a sound from inside. Had she said something to him?

The sound came again, and this time he heard the

distress in her voice. Nightmare? He tapped lightly on the door. "Jacqui? You okay?"

When there was no answer, he cracked the door open just to be sure she was all right, peeking through the opening into the darkened room. "Jacqui?"

She stirred restlessly against her pillows, making another soft but infinitely sad sound. Abandoning discretion, he moved across the room, sitting on the side of the bed to place a hand lightly on her face. "Jacqui. It's okay. You're dreaming."

He could just make out her face in the shadows. Her eyes opened, their depths glittering with unshed tears. She sounded dazed and disoriented when she said, "What?"

"You were dreaming," he repeated gently. "Sounded like a bad one. I just wanted to make sure you're okay."

She reached up to rub a hand over her face, swiping her cheeks as if to make sure they were dry. "I'm okay. I hope I didn't wake you."

"No, I was just passing your door on my way to bed. I wouldn't have even heard you if I'd been in my room."

"What time is it?"

He glanced at the clock. "Eleven-thirty. I've been outside chatting with Waldo."

Apparently, he'd sat outside longer than he had realized.

She drew a deep breath, and he was pleased to note that she sounded steadier now. "Go get some sleep, Mitch. I'm fine, thanks."

"Sure you don't want to talk about it?"

"I'm sure."

Still, he hated to leave her alone when he suspected

her hands were still trembling. "That incident with Alice tonight really rattled you, didn't it?"

"I was concerned," she replied a little stiltedly. "It was bad enough that she was out running around with a bunch of kids I don't really know, but it was really unlike her to be an hour later getting home than she agreed to."

"I know. She gave everyone a scare."

"I hope she won't do anything like that again."

He gave a little shrug. "I hope not, too, but I'm sure she'll misbehave at least a few more times before she's grown. Most teenagers do, even the best ones."

"Unfortunately, you're probably right." Jacqui shifted in the bed, pulling the sheet a little higher.

He supposed she was self-conscious at lying in the bed in her nightshirt with him sitting fully dressed gazing down at her. He really should let her go back to sleep—but he had to admit he was reluctant to leave. What he really wanted to do was crawl beneath that sheet with her, no longer fully dressed.

Instead, he asked a question he suspected she wouldn't really want him to ask. "Was a teen driver behind the wheel when your sister died?"

She went very still and, though it was difficult to be certain in the dim room, he thought he saw her pale in response to the clearly unexpected question. "Yes," she said after a taut pause.

"That's why you worry so much about Alice riding with teenagers."

"I would worry about that regardless."

"So would I. But I wondered if that was what triggered your nightmare. Were you dreaming about your sister?"

He wasn't sure she was going to answer. Finally, she

turned her face away from him and murmured, "Alice and Olivia were both in my dream. It was bad."

Mitch reached out to stroke a damp strand of hair from her face. "I'm sorry. I can't imagine how much it must still hurt you."

She looked up at him then with her chin lifted. He guessed that Jacqui didn't like to be seen looking so vulnerable. "It was just a nightmare, Mitch. I don't have them often. I'll be fine. Go get some sleep."

He nodded, then made himself stand. "All right. If you need anything, you know where to find me."

"Thank you. I appreciate your concern," she said, her too-formal tone making him smile.

He paused in the doorway to glance back toward the bed. "Jacqui? Just so you'll know, I'm not entirely noble. I was very tempted to climb into that bed with you."

"I was very tempted to ask you to," she replied after only a momentary pause.

He groaned. "Thanks for sharing that. Now I won't sleep tonight, either."

He thought he heard her laugh softly when he closed her door behind him. At least he'd left her smiling, he thought as he crossed the hall to his own lonely, borrowed bed. For a moment anyway. He would bet her smile had faded the moment he'd left her alone in the dark.

Pulling his shirt over his head, he tossed it onto a chair and reached for his belt buckle. He found it difficult to smile now. He kept hearing the echo of that soft, sad sound Jacqui had made in her tormented sleep.

It wasn't too much of a stretch to guess that Jacqui had been the teenage driver when her sister had died. And it killed him to think she was still carrying the guilt from that long-ago accident. Maybe it was the physician in him that wanted to do something to alleviate her pain—or maybe he was beginning to care too much about her. The problem was, he could repair a broken bone—but a broken heart was beyond his skills.

Although Jacqui slept only half an hour later than she usually arose, Mitch was gone by the time she woke, showered and dressed the next morning. She had to admit she was relieved. She wondered if he had deliberately slipped out before she got up to avoid any potential awkwardness from the night before.

It had definitely been a eventful evening, she thought, busying herself with housework in a futile attempt to keep herself from replaying every minute of last night. Heated, arousing kisses on the couch. The disturbing call from Alice's grandmother. The nightmare—still much too clear in her mind. Then waking to find Mitch sitting on her bed, his touch so gentle on her face that she'd had to forcibly stop herself from burrowing straight into his arms.

She wasn't accustomed to having anyone there when she woke after a bad dream. As much as she told herself she wasn't a child and didn't need to be comforted after a nightmare, it had still been nice to have someone stroke her and speak to her soothingly until the horrifying images faded. She could get used to that—which was an unsettling thought.

Maybe it was because of that dream in which she had lost both Olivia and Alice in the devastating car accident, but she couldn't be too angry with the girl when she returned home, chastened and wary. Her grandparents dropped her off. Jacqui invited them in for coffee, but they were in a hurry to return home. Jacqui noted that the couple parted affectionately with Alice, who saw them off with a murmured promise that she would never cause them worry again. Apparently, she'd gotten a good talking to from her grandparents—only a hint of what would come from her father, Jacqui thought with a twinge of sympathy.

"I'm not going to fuss at you anymore," she said after Alice had sullenly apologized to her again. "It's up to your dad to take it from here. All I'm going to say is that when you're left in my charge, you're going to have to follow my rules. You knew I wouldn't approve of you riding in a car with Milo, but you implied to your grandparents that Milo is a trusted friend of the family. That was both dishonest and dangerous, Alice."

"I know I should have been back when I said," Alice conceded, looking close to tears. "And I guess I shouldn't have been in the car with Milo. He drove sort of fast. I think he was showing off. I told him to slow down, but he just laughed. You won't tell Dad that part, will you?"

"I'm sure he was showing off in front of you girls." Jacqui swallowed hard at the thought of what could have happened with that boy driving recklessly with three young girls in his car. "I hope you at least wore your seat belt."

"Of course I wore my seat belt. I always do." Alice sounded ironically indignant that Jacqui would even suggest differently.

"As for telling your Dad, I think you should decide what to tell him when you talk with him about last night. But I would advise you to be honest and penitent about breaking his rules."

Alice sighed gustily. "All the other girls my age are allowed to go out."

"You're telling me Tiff's mother would let her go riding around with an almost-eighteen-year-old boy?"

Alice grimaced, as aware as Jacqui that her friend Tiffany's mother was every bit as firm and protective as Seth. "No, I guess not."

"You know not."

Alice merely sighed again.

"Why don't you go out and play with Waldo? He's missed you."

Alice escaped eagerly. Jacqui figured the girl was looking forward to spending time with her dog, who thought everything she did was perfectly delightful.

Later that afternoon, Jacqui debated awhile before knocking on Alice's bedroom door. Alice had been in there for more than an hour, having said she wanted to play on her computer and maybe read a little. Jacqui suspected Alice was still sulking, embarrassed by the fuss she had caused. Alice was also worried about what her father was going to say when he heard about the incident.

After being invited into the room, Jacqui opened the door and stepped inside. The teen lay sprawled on her bed on top of the comforter, an open book in front of her.

Jacqui crossed the room to perch on one corner of the bed. "How's the book?"

"Pretty good. It's the third in a series."

"That series about the rescue dogs?"

"Yeah. Guess I told you about them already."

"You mentioned them."

Closing the book, Alice sat up, her legs crossed in front of her. "What's that you're holding?"

"It's an old picture. I thought you might like to see it."

Alice waited a moment. When Jacqui didn't immediately hand her the photo, she prodded, "You were going to show me the picture?"

Taking a deep breath, Jacqui handed Alice the faded, creased photo. In it, two little girls, ages eight and ten, sat side by side on a concrete step eating ice cream cones. The older had dark hair rumpled in spikes around her solemn face, whereas the younger girl's hair was lighter, wavier, her expression blissful as she enjoyed the melting treat.

Frowning in concentration, Alice pointed to the older girl. "This is you, isn't it?"

"Yes. I guess I haven't changed much."

"You were very cute."

Jacqui smiled a little. "Thanks."

"Who's the other girl?"

The smile faded. "My sister. Olivia."

Alice's eyes went wide. "You never told me you have a sister."

"Had," Jacqui corrected gently. "I had a sister."

Alice bit her lip before asking, "She died?"

"Yes. From injuries she sustained in a car accident when she was only a little older than you are now. It will be twelve years ago next week."

Blinking rapidly, Alice looked down at the photograph again. "I'm sorry. She looks nice."

"She was."

"You must really miss her, huh?"

Jacqui took the photograph again, glancing down at it before replying, "Yes. I do."

"Is that why you freaked out that I was in a car with Milo?"

"Partly. I've seen the results of an inexperienced driver being distracted by passengers. I want you to stay safe, Alice. I want you to grow up to finish high school and go to prom and college and become an orthodontist or whatever you eventually decide to be. All the things Olivia never got to do. I'm not saying you should be covered in bubble wrap and never allowed to leave the house—tempting as that might be for your dad and for me—but I do think you should take reasonable precautions. Look both ways before you cross the street. Don't stand outside in a lightning storm. Wear a helmet when you ride your bike. And don't ride in a car with a reckless teenage boy who's showing off for a group of younger girls."

"Was Olivia riding in a car with a reckless teenage boy?" Alice asked, subdued.

"No." Folding her hand around the treasured photograph, Jacqui stood. "Just a driver who was too young to react quickly enough in a dangerous situation. I want you to understand why your family and I are so concerned about the ground rules they've developed for you, Alice. Your dad will probably chew you out when he gets here, but it's only because he wants you to stay safe. You'll get a little more freedom with each passing year, but I expect you'll have to demonstrate first that you're ready to take each new step."

"By not breaking the rules, you mean?"

Jacqui smiled. "That's definitely a good start."

She reached out to stroke a hand over Alice's soft, curly hair. "Don't dread your dad getting home, Alice. He'll fuss, but he'll be very happy to see you, too. He loves you very much. You know he can never stay mad at you for long."

"Thanks, Jacqui. And I'm sorry about your sister. Will you tell me about her sometime?"

"Sometime," Jacqui promised. "Not today."

"Okay." She set the book aside. "Maybe I'll go swim for a while. Do you want to swim with me?"

"I'll sit outside with you while you swim. I'd like to get some knitting time in before making dinner."

Leaving the girl to change, she walked to her own room to put away her photograph. She wasn't sure why she'd brought it out today. Maybe she was simply ready to talk about Olivia again. And maybe Mitch had something to do with that.

She and Mitch had shared a house for less than two weeks and already she felt as though some things in her world had shifted. She had been so content before—or so she'd convinced herself. She hated to think her life would be in any way less satisfying when this atypical interlude came to an inevitable end.

Chapter Nine

Seth and Meagan returned Thursday afternoon in a flurry of baggage and gifts and hugs. Alice threw herself happily into her father's loving arms, then gave her stepmother an equally fervent welcome-home hug. It had been only a couple of weeks since they'd all seen each other, and Jacqui was sure Seth and Meagan had enjoyed their rare time together, but they were obviously happy to be back home again.

Keeping one arm around his daughter's shoulders, Seth greeted Jacqui. "Well?" he teased. "You aren't holding a resignation letter behind your back, are you?"

She smiled. "No. We've gotten by just fine."

"Uh-huh." Seth had heard a little about his daughter's mini-rebellion over the phone—but not from Jacqui, who had left that task to Alice and her grandparents. He gave his daughter a look that promised a talk later, then hugged her again before releasing her.

Meagan smiled at Jacqui. "To add to your chores while we were gone, I hear you've also been taking care of my homeless brother. You certainly had your hands full, didn't you?"

Jacqui forced a smile. She'd hardly seen Mitch since he'd left her bedroom after her nightmare two nights earlier. He'd been busy at work—or maybe busy avoiding her once Alice was there to observe them. He hadn't talked to Alice about the incident at her grandparents' house, probably figuring there were enough adults on the girl's case about that, but instead had teased his niece just like always during the brief times they were both home. His manner toward Jacqui had been friendly, casual, deliberately proper in front of the girl. But the expression in his eyes when their glances had occasionally collided had let her know he hadn't forgotten one moment of the time they had spent alone together.

"It was no trouble at all," she assured Meagan, hoping no one could tell she was lying through her teeth.

Meagan smiled wryly. "Right. Thank you anyway for everything you've done."

"No problem." She figured she had earned every penny of the generous bonus she had been promised in her next paycheck.

A short while later, she left the family to catch up while she returned to her newly renovated apartment. She had the next three days off, and she planned to enjoy the leisure time. It would be nice to be responsible for no one but herself for the long weekend.

Her apartment smelled like new, cheap carpet and adhesive, but she saw at a glance that the work had been adequately done. What few possessions she'd left there were still intact. The new flooring and a few new furnishings made the inexpensive furnished rental look a little more updated than when she'd first moved in. There was even a new laminate countertop in the tiny galley kitchen, she noted in satisfaction. The old one had been in pretty bad shape.

Her rent would probably go up when the lease came up for renewal, she thought resignedly. She hoped it would still be reasonable. This was a decent place to live until she found a house she could afford, which would be at least one more lease cycle.

She unpacked and put everything away, then settled onto the new plaid couch with her knitting. Her TV was small and she had only very basic cable, so she didn't bother trying to find anything to watch. It was nice to just enjoy the quiet for a while.

It felt good to be back in her own place, she assured herself. Now that Seth and Meagan were home, everything could get back to normal. School would be starting again soon, and her days would settle back into a predictable routine of cleaning and shopping and laundry, picking up Alice after school, then cooking dinner for the family before returning here to her apartment. A comfortable, pleasant, generally stress-free schedule. Exactly the way she liked it.

Her sigh echoed in the silent room, making her frown in response to the plaintive sound.

"Stop being an idiot, Jacqui," she muttered, forcing herself to concentrate on the intricate pattern taking shape between her rapidly moving knitting needles.

Her phone rang a couple of times that afternoon. Her friend Alexis called to reschedule their previous lunch plans for the coming Saturday. "I promise I won't cancel on you this time. No matter what comes up, I'll tell everyone I already have plans."

Jacqui chuckled. "I'll look forward to it. It's been too long since we've managed to get together."

"I know. I want to hear everything you've been up to lately."

That wouldn't take long, Jacqui thought, wincing a little as she disconnected the call. She could tell Alexis a little about the past two weeks, but she wouldn't be comfortable sharing too much of the Llewellyn's personal business. As for anything that had happened between her and Mitch—well, she wasn't prepared to talk about that with her casual friend, either. She wasn't actually close enough to anyone with whom to discuss her complicated feelings for Mitch, she thought wistfully. That was the sort of intimate discussion best held between the very dearest of friends—or sisters, perhaps, she thought with a pang.

Oddly enough, she thought she could talk to LaDonna about her confused feelings, had the circumstances been a bit different. LaDonna always seemed so caring, so levelheaded and accepting. Jacqui wished she could feel as comfortable turning to her own mother as she would be to her employer's mom, if the current dilemma didn't involve LaDonna's own adored son.

Almost as if fate had intercepted that thought, the second call she received that afternoon was from her mother. Jacqui glanced at the caller ID screen with a wince, realizing that it had been almost two months since they'd last talked. "Hi, Mom. How are you and Dad?"

"We're doing well, thanks, sweetie. We're in Denver. We moved here last month and your dad has already found a good job doing maintenance for an apartment complex. I'm going to be helping out part-time in the rental office. In exchange, we get a free apartment and enough pay to provide the necessities. I think we'll be staying here for a while."

Jacqui had heard that before. She wondered exactly how long it would be before her father decided another pasture sounded greener. "That's great, Mom. I've heard Denver is a nice place to live. I hope you'll be happy there."

"You're still in Little Rock?"

"Yes. Still working for the same family. It's going well."

"I'm glad for you, sweetie. I know how you like your routines."

Jacqui frowned a little, wondering if she'd just been subtly patronized, but she decided to let it go. There was no reason for her to take offense by anything her long-distance parent said. "Yes, I'm quite content here," she said simply.

"Maybe you could take a vacation soon? Come to Denver to see your Dad and me? It's been a long time since we've been together, you know."

"I have got some vacation time coming. I'll try to get out there for a few days."

Assuming, of course, her parents were still in Denver when she took her planned two-week vacation time in October, a month she had chosen because it was a fairly slow time in the Llewellyn household. She wasn't enthusiastic about digging into her savings for airfare, but she supposed she should make an effort to see her parents at least once every year or so, and it had been more than a year since the last visit.

"Oh, that would be wonderful. I know your dad will be happy to see you. And so will I."

"I'll do my best."

"Our apartment is only one bedroom, but we have

a nice couch. You won't mind sleeping on that, will you?"

"Of course not." It wouldn't be the first time she'd slept on a couch—or a pallet on the floor, for that matter. Her parents hadn't always been able to provide enough beds for the four of them.

"So, what's been going on with you? Are you seeing anyone special?"

"Not really. But I have friends. And I stay busy. It's a good life."

"Well—I'm glad. You, um, you know next week is—"

Her mother's voice faded, but Jacqui was able to finish the sentence in her head. Next week was the anniversary of her sister's death. She hadn't needed that reminder. "Yes, I know."

"She would want you to be happy, sweetie. We all want that for you."

"And I am, thanks, Mom. I hope you and Dad are, too."

"We're getting by," her mother replied vaguely. "I should probably go. We thought we'd go out for a little while this evening. There's a nice little tavern nearby. Good music, nice people. We stop in occasionally for a drink."

Probably more than occasionally, Jacqui thought, but that was their business, not hers. "Okay, well, have a good time."

"We will, sweetie. Thanks. Um—talk to you soon?"

"Sure. I'll let you know when I finalize my vacation plans."

"I'd like that. I— Goodbye, Jacqui."

"'Bye, Mom."

Tossing the phone aside, she shoved a suddenly weary

hand through her hair. She couldn't help thinking of the lively conversations she'd overheard in the Llewellyn and Baker households—all the teasing and squabbling and I-love-yous. She did love her parents, she mused somberly, but such expressions of emotion had never been easy for them.

She glanced at her watch. Almost 6:00 p.m. She wasn't really hungry, but she was too restless to sit any longer with her knitting. Setting the project aside, she rose, glancing toward the little kitchen across the room. She'd stopped by the grocery store on the way home, so she had a few things to prepare. Maybe she'd see if anything looked appetizing.

She had taken only a couple of steps in that direction when someone knocked on her door. Blinking in surprise, she turned. She was popular today, she thought, wondering who was dropping by unannounced. Probably the landlord, making sure everything was satisfactory. He'd been very grateful for her patience during the renovation; because she'd had another place to stay, she hadn't pressed for immediate action as she was sure some of her neighbors had done.

Glancing through the peephole from force of long habit, she swallowed a groan and rested her head against the door for a moment before opening it. So much for the relaxing, decision-free evening she had envisioned.

"Hello, Mitch."

He stood in the open doorway, searching her face as if to decipher her reaction to his surprise call. "Hi. I got away from work a little earlier than usual today. I hope this isn't a bad time for me to drop by."

Without answering, she moved aside to let him in, closing the door behind him before turning to look at him. He was the one who'd shown up at her home out of the blue; she figured it was up to him to start whatever conversation he'd come here to have.

She was aware that her apartment was hardly luxurious, especially in comparison to the places they had toured last Saturday. She'd never visited his duplex, but it had probably been more upscale than this little furnished rental. Still, she refused to be self-conscious about her modest surroundings. The apartment was clean, the neighborhood lower income but relatively safe, and she could easily afford the rent and still put away savings every month. It worked for her.

His mouth quirked, as though he was amused by her rather challenging silence. "Okay if I sit down?"

So maybe she wasn't being the most gracious hostess. That was his fault for showing up without an invitation, she told herself, even as she relented. "Of course. Have a seat. Can I get you anything? I can make coffee."

He chuckled. "There you go again. You aren't on the job now, Jacqui. No need to use your Mary Poppins voice."

"Mary Poppins wasn't a housekeeper—she was a nanny," she muttered, vaguely embarrassed.

His grin widened. "Sorry. You're the one who's always making movie analogies. Guess I'm not as good at it."

His teasing was making her relax a bit, as he probably intended. She motioned toward the couch. "Sit down, Mitch. Tell me why you're here."

Catching her hand, he tugged her down beside him when he took a seat. "I think you know why I'm here."

She moistened her lips. "Not entirely," she said honestly.

He reached out to toy with the ends of her short hair,

a gesture that appeared to be becoming a habit for him. It seemed little more than an excuse to brush his fingers against her cheek, leaving trails of sensation behind. "Because I can't stay away from you."

All the differences between them flashed through her mind, all the reasons why this was such a bad idea.

He searched her face, probably trying to read her emotions. "We're on your turf now," he reminded her. "All you have to do is ask me to leave and I will. No argument."

Despite all her qualms, all her logical, sensible warnings to herself, she simply couldn't make herself utter the words that would send him away. Not tonight. She sighed lightly and leaned toward him. "Don't go," she murmured.

He had her in his arms, his mouth on hers, before she'd even finished speaking.

Neither of them was in a hurry. Jacqui, for one, had nowhere else to be. Tonight they didn't have to worry about discretion; they had complete privacy here in her apartment. They took full advantage of that freedom.

They left his shirt on the couch when they moved toward the bedroom. His shoes were shed somewhere along the way. By the time they reached her bed, her jeans were on the floor. His mouth seeking hers again, Mitch reached for the hem of her knit top.

She had only a momentary qualm before she raised her arms to allow him to tug the shirt over her head. It wasn't entirely modesty that gave her pause. Mitch's gaze zoomed straight to the reason she had hesitated.

His touch was so very gentle when he traced the scar that crossed her abdomen. "Spleen?"

"Gone."

"The accident?"

"Yes." She had spent six weeks recovering physically from that surgery. She would never fully recover emotionally, although the pain had lessened somewhat with time.

She had to be careful of infections and take a few routine precautions, but otherwise, she could live a full, normal life without a spleen. A doctor had told her after the surgery that she was fortunate to have lost only that relatively unnecessary organ. Still half-crazed with guilt and grief, she had screamed at him that he was an idiot. She had lost so much more than a spleen in that accident.

Catching her face between his hands, Mitch brushed his lips across hers, the kiss so sweet, so tender that it brought a lump to her throat. His mouth moved lightly across her cheek and down her throat, his hands exploring her back with long, smooth strokes that were as arousing as they were soothing. Lowering her to the bed, he kissed her throat and then the rise of her breasts above her white lace bra. He touched his lips to the scar before returning to capture her mouth, unfastening her bra as he did so.

She was not busty, but he seemed to approve of the way her breasts fit into his hands. His thumbs rotated lazily, and she arched with a gasp of reaction. It had been a while since she had allowed anyone this access, since there had been anyone with whom she had wanted to share these intimacies. Her rapidly overheating body was letting her know just how much she needed this release.

Mitch had come prepared for lovemaking. She decided to wonder later if he'd been so confident that she would invite him to stay, or if he had simply hoped she would. Whatever the reason, for now she could only be grateful.

For all the reasons she had listed earlier of why they were so poorly matched, they were certainly an ideal fit physically. Their bodies moved together, meshed together as perfectly as if they'd been built as a set. Once again, she sensed no awkwardness or hesitance between them. Sure, there was a giddy, first-time excitement— and yet an odd familiarity at the same time, a sensation she had felt with him before. If she were the fanciful, romantic type, she would imagine they were meant to be together. Fortunately, she was more sensible than that, she thought, even as she drew him closer.

They climaxed together, their soft cries sounding in perfect harmony.

Propped on one elbow, Mitch gazed down at Jacqui as she lay beside him, both slowly recovering their strength. He loved touching her hair, he mused, brushing a strand from her flushed face. It was so soft and thick, the cute, choppy cut tickling his fingers. Some guys were obsessed with long hair, but he thought Jacqui's style was perfect to best display her graceful neck and the pretty face highlighted by those big, dark eyes that could so easily mesmerize him.

He loved touching her skin, too, he thought as he allowed his fingers to slide down her throat to her shoulder. So warm and smooth and taut over her slender, toned body. The occasional splatter of golden freckles enchanted him. The scar that bisected her firm abdomen saddened him but made her no less attractive to him.

She opened her eyes and gazed up at him. Her expressions were becoming more readable to him, he thought optimistically. He thought he saw the lingering signs

of pleasure there, physical satisfaction—and maybe a
hint of the misgivings that were probably creeping back
into her mind now that they had satisfied their desire for
each other. Temporarily satisfied, he corrected himself,
knowing he would soon want her again.

"Are you hungry?" she asked, her voice still a bit
huskier than usual. "I could make you something."

He almost told her that she was so damned cute, but
he suspected that would get him punched—and she had
access to a few too many vulnerable places at the moment. Instead, he teased lightly, "Always trying to feed
me."

She shrugged against the pillows, her own lips twitch-
ing. "That's what I do."

"You're very good at it," he assured her with mock
solemnity. "You're very good at everything you do," he
added, dropping a kiss on the end of her nose.

He was delighted when she giggled, the sound so rare
he couldn't help laughing in response.

"Why, thank you, sir. But you still haven't answered
me. Are you hungry?"

"Not really." He was perfectly content to just lie there
for a while, savoring the aftermath of the best sex he'd
had in…well, ever. "Are you?"

She shook her head. "No."

"Then maybe we could just talk for a while."

He saw the faintest hint of nerves cross her face in response to his suggestion. He wouldn't have been able to
detect that a couple weeks ago. He liked to think he was
getting to know her better despite her reservations.

"We don't have to talk about anything that makes you
uncomfortable," he assured her. "We can chat about the
weather, if you want. I just enjoy being with you."

She smiled. "We don't have to chat about the weather.

For one thing, that's too boring in Arkansas in August. Hot and dry with a chance of afternoon thunderstorms. Pretty much sums it up."

Chuckling, he nodded. "Yeah, pretty much. Gets kind of boring, huh?"

She didn't respond, exactly, but asked, instead, "What will the weather be like in Peru?"

He wasn't sure what had made her think of his upcoming trip. "Somewhat cooler. It's winter there, you know."

"Yes."

"I wish you could go with me. I guess it's too late to make the arrangements."

She frowned, obviously startled by his impulsive comment. "Go with you? To Peru?"

"It's going to be a fun trip. Lots of hiking and sightseeing. I'd enjoy sharing it with you."

"Like you said, it's too late to make arrangements for that."

He wondered if he heard a hint of relief in her voice that she wouldn't be forced to make that decision.

"Anyway, I've already made a commitment, sort of, for my upcoming vacation," she said a bit too offhandedly. "My mother called earlier. She wants me to visit her and my dad in Denver for a few days."

"They're living in Denver now?"

"Yes. Managing an apartment complex there. She said they like it."

"Was that one of the places you lived with them?"

"No. They've only been there a month."

"Think they'll stay there?"

She sighed almost imperceptibly. "Who knows? I wouldn't be entirely surprised if I get a call saying they've moved on before I can even make plane reservations."

"Did you have a good talk with your mom?"

"The usual. She told me what they were up to, asked if I'm still in the same place, called me boring, then asked me to come visit."

He lifted an eyebrow in response to one item on that list. "Your mother called you boring?"

"Well…maybe not in so many words," she admitted.

"What words did she use?"

"She said that I've always liked my daily routines."

He thought about that for a moment before asking, "Well? Don't you?"

Her own pause was a bit longer. "Yeah. I guess I do," she muttered. "It was just the way she said it…made it sound so dull."

Mitch laughed. "Trust me, Jacqui. There is nothing dull about you."

She looked pleased by the compliment. "Thanks."

He tapped her chin with one finger. "You're welcome."

Looking at him through her lashes, she said, "My mother reminded me that next week is the anniversary of my sister's death. An unnecessary reminder, of course."

"Do your parents blame you for the accident that killed your sister?" He took a risk asking, but he really wanted to know.

She stiffened a little. "I never said I was driving."

He merely looked at her.

Jacqui sighed. "I guess it was obvious. I was driving. I'd had my license for less than a month, and had little formal training behind the wheel. Dad just handed me the keys and told me to go get Olivia and me something to eat because he and Mom had other things to do. They planned to spend the evening in a bar close to the motel where we were living, just outside Chicago. A teenager in a sports car ran a red light and hit the old car I was driving, right in the passenger door. I've already told you Olivia died on the operating table. I damaged my spleen and had a few broken bones, but she took the brunt of the crash."

"How old were you?"

"I was almost seventeen. Olivia had just turned fifteen."

"And you blame yourself? Even though the other teen driver ran the light?"

"I don't blame myself, exactly. The boy was at fault. But if I'd been more experienced, maybe a little less distracted by something Olivia was saying or by trying to decide where to eat…"

"You do blame yourself. That's a heavy burden to carry, Jacqui."

"I carried it a long time," she admitted. "I've learned to let it go. Most of the time."

"The other driver—was he injured?"

"Yes. He had a head injury that was expected to cause him lifelong challenges. I don't know how he's done since, haven't really wanted to find out. It was a tragedy for him and his family, too. He was just a pampered kid, driving too fast in a car that was too powerful for a boy his age. Some friends were following him in another car, and he was showing off for them. They're the ones who called the paramedics."

"It must have been a horrible time for you and your parents."

"It was. His insurance covered the hospital bills and

the funeral and supported my parents for a couple of years, but it couldn't soothe the pain of their loss."

"Or yours."

"No."

He suspected that Jacqui hadn't received a penny of that money, other than to pay her hospital bills. "What happened after that? With you and your family, I mean?"

"After a few months, Dad needed to move on. Running, that time. Mom started packing, the way she always does, but I told them I'd had enough of wandering aimlessly from place to place. I was ready to find someplace and stay awhile. I found a job at a restaurant, and I stayed behind when they left. It was the best choice for all of us."

"And you were seventeen?"

"Yes."

"Still so young."

"I've always been old for my age."

She'd had reason to be, he thought, guessing from some of the things she'd said about her parents that she must have been placed in charge of her younger sister from the time she was quite young. Which would have made her feel even more responsible for Olivia's death. "I'm very sorry about what you've been through, Jacqui."

She shook her head impatiently. "Other than losing my sister, I haven't had such a bad life. My parents have their faults, but they never treated us badly. I've had jobs I liked, met some great people in my travels—like the sweet neighbor who taught me how to knit when I was a kid and my friend who owns the boutique and sells my work there. I have a couple of good friends here— I'm having lunch with my friend Alexis this Saturday.

I liked my last job for Mr. Avery in Hot Springs, and I love working for your sister's family. I have nothing, really, to complain about, though I do miss Olivia, of course."

She was so determined not to be pitied. He understood her well enough by now to know she valued her competence and independence, and he couldn't blame her for that. She'd been on her own a long time—even before that physical separation from her parents, he thought. She'd made her own way in the world and had done so quite successfully. She deserved to take pride in that.

"You know, I think I am hungry after all." She rolled abruptly and reached for her clothes. "I'll take the bathroom first. You can wash up while I cook."

He lay on his back, his arms akimbo behind his head. "Take your time."

He would just lie here for a while longer, thinking about some of the things she had said and wondering where they would go from here.

Chapter Ten

Jacqui felt as though she were living a double life. She continued to report to work at the usual time and performed her usual duties once there. She cleaned and did laundry, chauffeured Alice for some back-to-school shopping, wrestled Waldo into the car for a visit to the vet for his annual shots, ran errands and cooked dinners for the family before leaving every evening. She doubted that anyone in the family had any suspicion at all that her life had changed dramatically during the past week.

She saw Mitch nearly every day. Saying he thought it was better for all concerned, he'd moved out of his sister's house the day after Meagan and Seth returned from their trip. His mother had urged him to stay with her, but he'd chosen instead to check into a hotel near the hospital until he could make more permanent arrangements. He'd told his mother that he didn't want to disturb her with his erratic work hours, but Jacqui knew he had moved into the hotel so no one knew he was spending most of his free time with her.

She had made him promise not to tell anyone they were spending time together. Much less that they had become lovers. Although he'd argued that he didn't care who knew he was seeing Jacqui, he had conceded to her request. He thought she was putting off telling everyone because she needed time to adjust to the change in their relationship. Time to get used to thinking of them as a couple before letting anyone else see them that way.

What would he think, she wondered, if he knew she was keeping their affair a secret because she fully expected it to be short-lived and hoped to avoid as much awkwardness as possible when it inevitably ended? Would he accuse her of conceding defeat before they even had a chance to make it work, or would he secretly appreciate that she was trying to spare him discomfort with his family?

As much as she was trying to protect her heart, she knew she was going to miss him badly if—when—this all ended. The physical part of their relationship was amazing. Addictive. Like nothing she had ever experienced before. But even more, she savored the interludes afterward when they lay snuggled together in her bed, talking about their days or whatever else popped into their heads.

He made her laugh with stories from his childhood, and she found herself telling him little anecdotes from her own, something she never did with other people. They talked about his adventures—and misadventures—with his sisters, and she told him some of the scrapes she and Olivia had gotten into. It didn't hurt so much to talk about Olivia with Mitch, she discovered. Maybe because he knew how her sister had died and didn't seem to judge her for it. Maybe because finally breaking her silence about Olivia with both Mitch and Alice made each mention of her a little easier.

Or maybe it was just that Mitch was incredibly easy to talk to.

They didn't talk much about the future. She supposed he was doing something about finding a permanent place to live, but he didn't discuss it. Mostly, when they looked ahead, it was not beyond Mitch's rapidly approaching trip to Peru. He was so excited about that trek. She hoped it would be as much fun as he thought it would be. He would be so disappointed if it wasn't.

She was going to miss him while he was away. But then, who knew if they'd still be together by the time he left anyway, she reminded herself. She wasn't making any plans. She was simply going to enjoy it while it lasted. And when it ended—well, she had a lot of experience with moving on. She could still be friendly enough with Mitch on the rare occasions they would see each other through his family. And no one else would ever have to know about their temporary insanity.

The end came even sooner than she had predicted.

They had been lovers for just more than a week when Mitch reluctantly dressed to leave her apartment Monday night. It wasn't all that late, but he had an early surgery the next morning. He thought it best that he go back to the hotel for a few hours of sleep first. He lingered for quite a while at the door as one good-night kiss led to another—and then another.

Finally she drew herself out of his arms and stepped back, warding him off when he laughingly reached for her again. "Go," she ordered. "Get some sleep."

"I'm going." He heaved a sigh. "It gets harder to leave."

"You're just tired of that hotel."

"That, too." He opened the door, then paused in the doorway as if a thought had just occurred to him. "Jacqui—Madison's birthday is next weekend."

Lifting an eyebrow, she nodded. "I know. Meagan and Alice mentioned that they're going shopping tomorrow evening to find her a gift."

"We're having a get-together at Mom's Saturday night. Casual. Just family."

She felt the muscles in her chest tighten as he spoke, making it more difficult to breathe. "Mitch—"

"Go with me, Jacqui. Everyone would love to have you there."

As a matter of fact, LaDonna had already invited her. Jacqui hadn't yet given an answer. She had wanted first to confirm with Mitch that they could both attend the party without giving anyone a hint of their true relationship. Now she wasn't so sure.

"You're, um, asking me to be there—just as a guest of the family?"

"As my guest," he corrected. "I'd like us to go together."

Twisting her hands in the tie of her short terry robe, she shook her head. "I don't think that's a good idea. Everyone would start wondering what's going on. You know Madison, especially, would be asking questions. Right now everyone thinks we're just friends, but if we start attending parties together, they're going to get different ideas."

"The right idea, you mean."

"We're not ready for that to come out yet." If ever.

"You're not ready. Frankly, I don't see the need for

all the secrecy. I mean, sure, it was nice to have this past week all to ourselves without any outside scrutiny, but it's inevitable that people are going to find out. What better time to make the announcement than when everyone's already gathered together?"

It must have been panic that made her blurt tactlessly, "Make what announcement? That you're sleeping with your sister's housekeeper?"

As soon as she said them, she wished she could call the words back. Not because they weren't what she was thinking, but because they led to a line of discussion she wasn't sure she was ready to get into tonight.

Mitch closed the door deliberately. Planting his hands on his hips, he frowned at her. "Considering that you are a very intelligent woman, that was a really dumb thing to say."

She flushed a little but lifted her chin and stood her ground. "Maybe. But still true. Why does everyone need to know our private business?"

"Because I don't want to get in a position of lying to my family. Or sneaking around behind their back with you. Look, I know it's still very early in our relationship..."

"We don't have a relationship, Mitch. We're just having a little fun for now while you're at loose ends with your future plans, and there's nothing at all wrong with that, but there's no need for everyone to know about it. I don't want anything to change between me and the rest of your family, once you and I— You know."

"After we stop sleeping together?" he asked a bit too politely.

She shrugged.

"You never intended to give this a real chance, did you?"

"You're the one who said you're not at a point in your life where you're interested in long-term leases," she reminded him.

"That's hardly fair. I was talking about real estate, not us."

She shook her head sadly. "Don't you see, Mitch? It's all tied up together. I *am* the type who wants a long-term lease once I find exactly what I'm looking for. I don't mind an occasional short-term stay in a decent place while I'm searching for a permanent home, but I always know going in that it's only temporary."

He looked baffled by her tangled analogy, and she supposed she couldn't blame him for that. Still, she thought maybe he'd gotten the message. When it came to giving her heart, it was all or nothing with her. Until she found someone who felt exactly the same way—if that ever happened—she was keeping that vulnerable organ locked safely away. Even if it hadn't been for all the other obstacles between them, Mitch had made it clear enough during the past couple of weeks that he wasn't looking for long-term commitments.

"I love my job, and I don't want to ruin my relationship with your sisters and your mother," she repeated quietly. "I'm very fond of them. When you're off exploring Peru or looking for exciting new jobs in places other than where you've lived all your life, I'll still be here with them. I don't want them feeling as though they have to take sides between us or treat me any differently than they have before. I'm Meagan and Seth's housekeeper, an occasional nanny for Alice—and, for now anyway, a friend of the family. I'm content for things to stay that way."

"So it's a no on the party."

Her heart twisted in response to his expression

because they both knew she was turning down more than a simple invitation.

She agreed somewhat sadly. "It's a no."

He looked as though there was more he wanted to say, but he merely stood there for a moment in silence before he said, "Fine."

"I'll make an excuse to your mother. Other plans."

He nodded. "Whatever you want to tell her. I won't cause you any problems. I'd better go." He reached for the doorknob again. "I'll, uh, call you."

Knotting the robe tie more tightly around her bloodless fingers, she managed a faint smile. "Right."

He took one step outside her apartment, then paused once again. "Jacqui?" he said without looking back. "For the record—your job has never been an issue with me. I think you're damned good at it."

Despite her pain, it was still nice to hear him say that. "Thank you, Mitch."

"Good night." He closed the door behind him.

Moving forward to turn the locks, she sighed heavily. He had said "good night," but she thought she heard an echo of "goodbye" in her now-silent apartment.

She walked slowly over to the couch, where she sank onto one end and automatically picked up her knitting. She wouldn't be sleeping for a while yet, so she might as well be productive while she sat there brooding.

So, it hadn't lasted very long at all. Just over a week. Even with her brief history of ill-fated relationships, that was a record.

It was probably best this way. Short enough so that every moment had been close to perfection, at least until the very end. They hadn't had to deal with fights or makeups or conflicts of time or priorities that inevitably caused friction in long-term relationships. Because it had been so brief, and so private, she wouldn't have to deal with other people's sympathy or advice or disapproval. And because her routines had been disrupted for only a few days, it wouldn't take her long to fall back into them. She had been satisfied with her life before Mitch literally stumbled into it; she would be again, she promised herself.

It hadn't escaped her notice that he hadn't taken issue with her reminder that he wasn't looking for a long-term commitment. She hadn't expected a declaration of undying love or a flowery proposal of marriage—not after only a week of being together, certainly—but he could have argued that he was open to the possibilities. That he, too, was only waiting to be sure he'd found the right one before he made any binding promises.

Only he wasn't looking for commitment. Not now. Not when he was still nagged by curiosity about what lay beyond the borders of his first thirty-one years. He'd known commitment all his life—to his family, his education and career training, his job. She didn't really blame him for not wanting to tie himself to another anchor.

It was a good thing she had protected herself, she thought, glaring fiercely down at her knitting needles. Had she not, she would be in a great deal of pain right now. She would probably be feeling as if her tidy, carefully organized world had just crashed around her ears.

It was a very good thing she wasn't feeling that way now, she thought with a hard, aching swallow.

A worried couple awaited him when Mitch walked into a small, private hospital consultation room late Friday afternoon. They held hands as they watched him enter, followed closely by a surgical resident, who closed the door behind them. Mitch gave the parents a reassuring smile, offering his hand to each before inviting them to have a seat at the small, rectangular table in the cubicle-size room.

Sitting across from them, the resident seated quietly and observantly nearby, Mitch asked, "You were told that Jeffrey did very well during his surgery?"

"Yes, the volunteer and the nurse kept us updated," Laura Dickerson assured him, her voice quivering just a little with nerves. "There were none of the possible complications you warned us about?"

"No, everything went just fine."

No matter how many times he had done it, it always felt good to see the relief in worried parents' eyes when he consulted with them after successful operations. Just as it always grieved him to have to report otherwise. Fortunately, in his specialty he didn't have to relay heartbreaking news often. And in this particular case, the report was all good.

"I was able to cut his tibia and fibula very close to the growth plate, and the bones realigned very well. He'll have to wear the fixator I attached for between eight and twelve weeks, and he'll have physical therapy three times a week. We'll have to make adjustments in the fixator during the process and then evaluate at the end of three months to determine if any further corrections are necessary. It's going to be a challenging time for the whole family, but when it's all over, Jeffrey's legs will be as straight and strong as your own. You'll be racing to keep up with him again."

The three-year-old had been presented to Mitch with Blount's disease affecting his left leg, which had bowed during growth, making it somewhat shorter than his right leg. It hadn't been the worst case Mitch had seen by far, but he knew any procedure was drastic to the child's adoring parents. He expected young Jeffrey to benefit significantly from the operation Mitch had just performed, leading a full, active life afterward. That was just one of the reasons Mitch loved this job.

Fifteen minutes later, after answering a dozen questions and offering a dozen more reassurances, he left the conference room, gave the eager resident a list of instructions, then headed for his office. At least something in his life was going right, he thought as weariness gradually overpowered satisfaction. He hadn't been sleeping well this week. He'd been on call Wednesday night, and it had been a long one, leaving him drained and grumpy. Okay, so maybe there were times he didn't love his job so much. That was normal, too.

He was greeted by quite a few coworkers on the way to his office. He'd made a lot of friends here, he thought. He passed a couple of parents of young surgical patients, returning their greetings with friendly nods. He was accustomed to the respectful manner with which he was often treated—after all, these people had literally placed their children's well-being in his hands. He never wanted to let himself take that trust for granted or to let himself get jaded to the jumbled emotions his patients and their families had to deal with during medical crises.

Accepting a stack of messages from his always-organized secretary, he carried them into his office and tossed them onto his cluttered desk before falling into his chair. He had calls to return, reports to file, dictation to do—but it could all wait for just a minute, he thought, scrubbing his hands over his face.

"Here. Looked like you could use this."

His secretary placed a steaming cup of coffee on his

desk and gave him a sympathetic smile before returning to her own work.

Gratefully, he sipped the freshly brewed beverage, thinking he really should buy her some flowers or something. She'd gone beyond the call of duty during the past month. He hoped she knew how much he appreciated how efficiently she kept his professional life running, his schedule straight, his correspondence completed. Glancing at the door she had closed behind her, he wished fleetingly that he could turn over all his problems to her and have her handle them with the same firm hand.

Maybe then he could go to bed again without lying awake wondering why he had let Jacqui send him away. Wondering if he should have fought harder to hang on to something that had been so special. Wondering what kind of an idiot walked away from a woman like that just because she had very bravely and honestly informed him that she was the long-term-commitment type.

Hadn't he really known that all along? She'd certainly made it clear from the start that she'd had enough of drifting in her rootless childhood. She'd told him she was saving for a home of her own—and he had seen the pure lust on her face when they'd toured that Craftsman-style house in Hillcrest. Unlike him, Jacqui knew exactly what she wanted, and she was pursuing it with single-minded determination. He wished he had her clear-sightedness, her certainty of what it would take to make her happy.

With a wince, he remembered the way she had compared him to a short-term lease while she looked for a place to settle for the duration. Her words had been blunt, a little jumbled, but ultimately effective. He'd gotten the message clearly enough. She wasn't willing to settle. Wasn't willing to risk too much on a guy who wasn't prepared to offer forever.

What she hadn't said was whether she would be interested if he did want to spend the rest of his life with her. Was he no more to her than another furnished apartment—nice enough to spend some time there while she looked for the place she really wanted?

Another real estate metaphor, he thought, muttering an exasperated curse. But apt enough to make his shoulders sag in despairing self-recrimination.

He never wanted to hurt Jacqui. He'd do anything to prevent that—even stay far away from her, if that was what she wanted. But apparently he'd left more behind than he'd realized when he'd walked away. Judging from the emptiness inside him, he'd left a sizable piece of his heart. Did he have the courage to offer her the rest of it? And would she even accept it if he did?

Heaving a long sigh, he turned his focus to his work. As always, he had a stack of responsibilities waiting for his attention.

Jacqui tried to ignore the guilt she felt while sitting across the kitchen table from LaDonna Baker, sharing tea and cookies on Wednesday afternoon, eleven days after Jacqui had broken up with Mitch. Not that there had been much to break up, she told herself as she toyed with a cookie she didn't really want, just to have something to do with her hands during this visit.

LaDonna had dropped by with a pretty top for Alice that she'd found on a sale rack that afternoon. "I couldn't resist it," she'd admitted to Jacqui. "The color will look so pretty on Alice."

Unfortunately, Alice wasn't there to accept the gift. School was already in session during this final week of

August, having started Monday morning. After school, Alice would be competing in her last swim match of the season. Seth had arranged to attend that match, then he and Alice planned to meet Meagan for dinner, so Jacqui would be headed home soon. No one to cook for tonight but herself, she thought. Maybe she'd order a pizza and watch a little TV. That sounded like a perfectly nice evening. She wished she could look forward to it a little more.

Jacqui had invited LaDonna in for a snack and a chat, and the older woman had eagerly agreed. She didn't work on Wednesdays and it was sometimes difficult to entertain herself, she confessed. But maybe she had overdone it a bit that day. She was tired from her shopping excursion, and tea and a chat sounded like a lovely way to recuperate.

"You'd think I'd be over empty nest syndrome by now," she said as they lingered over the tea. "After all, my youngest child turned twenty-eight last week."

LaDonna's house had been empty only since last November, when she'd lost her mother, who had lived with her for several years. Jacqui thought it wasn't so unusual that LaDonna's home still felt empty to her at times after living there so long with her late husband, her now-grown children and then her mother. It must be difficult to make that transition from a full house to a quiet one. And LaDonna was still relatively young. It was no wonder she sometimes felt at loose ends.

"Did you buy anything for yourself during your shopping trip?" Jacqui asked.

"No," LaDonna admitted. "Just the top for Alice and that bag I described to you for Madison. Oh, and I got a lovely set of hand towels for a nice young couple from my church who is getting married next month. Half off, plus I had an extra-fifteen-percent coupon," she boasted.

Jacqui laughed. "Congratulations."

"I saw lots of nice things I thought Mitch could use, but because he can't seem to make up his mind if he's going to buy or rent his next place I wasn't sure exactly what he'd need. It's been five weeks since his duplex burned, and I know that's not a lot of time, but still, he should be making some progress in deciding what he wants. I swear, all that boy can think about is his work and his upcoming trip to Peru."

It took all her fortitude for Jacqui to keep smiling and speak lightly. "He's still very excited about that trip, I suppose."

"Well, yes."

Something in LaDonna's tone made Jacqui's eyebrows rise. "That didn't sound very certain."

"It's just that—well, he was so excited up until a week or so ago. Now he just seems distracted all the time. And he looks so tired. I guess he's been working like crazy to clear his schedule for the time off. I fussed at him over the phone yesterday, told him he's going to have to start getting some rest. Which would be easier, I said, if he were sleeping someplace other than a hotel. I wish he'd just move in with me while he makes his decision."

"I suppose he doesn't want to cause you any trouble," Jacqui replied, feeling guilty again that she was keeping so much from LaDonna.

Did Mitch miss her as much as she missed him? Did he, too, lie awake remembering the nights they had spent together and aching for more? Did he also wish things could have been different for them?

"As if having my son as a guest would be any trouble," LaDonna fretted.

Leaving her cookie untouched, she took a sip of her tea. Her pale face was creased with a frown when she lowered the cup. "Jacqui, do you have an ibuprofen available? I have a little headache."

Jacqui stood and moved to the cabinet where she kept a bottle of over-the-counter pain reliever. "Headache? Is that something you have often?"

"More often during the past few months," LaDonna admitted. "They seem to be getting worse. I suppose I should see someone about it."

Jacqui frowned at the older woman in concern. "With three doctors in your family, I'd have thought you'd have mentioned it to one of them."

"I hate to bother them with medical questions. They get enough of that at work. My annual physical is next month, so I'll mention it to my doctor then."

"I hope I'm not being too personal, but I've been a little worried about your health lately," Jacqui admitted, reaching for the high shelf where she stored the bottle. "You seem to have lost some weight and you look a little pale to me. I've been wanting to mention it, but I wasn't sure you'd—"

Her voice trailed into shocked silence when she saw LaDonna slumped in the chair. Throwing the plastic bottle of ibuprofen on the counter, she rushed forward. "LaDonna? *LaDonna!*"

Chapter Eleven

Mitch didn't know what his family would have done without Jacqui during the next three days. When he and his sisters and Alice reacted with panic to his mother's collapse and subsequent rush to the E.R., Jacqui remained calm, her soothing manner and outward confidence helping them all to remain optimistic.

It was Jacqui who had reacted so quickly to get his mother to the hospital and who had called each of them to give them the news of her illness. The first fear had been that LaDonna had suffered a heart attack. Instead, she was diagnosed as severely anemic, which led to the discovery of previously untreated bleeding stomach ulcers.

When the family reeled in shock from that news, Jacqui pointed out that LaDonna was in an excellent facility with highly skilled physicians and surgeons to care for her. When guilt and stress caused the physician siblings to snap at each other, mostly over who should have seen the signs that their mother had probably been ill for several months, Jacqui stepped in quickly to play peacemaker. She handled the brief conflict so skillfully that they were soon apologizing and working together to make the best medical decisions for their mother.

Jacqui fetched coffee and bottled waters, made phone calls, nagged everyone to eat and rest and served as a buffer when well-intentioned friends flooded them with calls and visits during the first hours after LaDonna's hospitalization. When Mitch's mom insisted that no one should miss work or school to sit in the hospital room with her while she recuperated enough to be discharged, Jacqui made them all feel more comfortable about leaving by offering to stay in their place. She promised to call each one if problems occurred. All of them checked on their mom every chance they got, but Mitch, for one, was able to concentrate better on his work knowing Jacqui was staying with her. He was sure the others felt the same way.

Jacqui had tried to warn him that his mother hadn't seemed well to her during the past few weeks, but he had basically brushed her off. He regretted that deeply now. Under questioning from her doctors and family, LaDonna admitted that she'd had some pain for several months, but had treated herself with over-the-counter medications. She had taken a lot of ibuprofen for stress headaches during her mother's long illness, she confessed on further questioning. Taking too much of the drug was associated with the formation of stomach ulcers.

There had been other symptoms, she said now. Long accustomed to caring for others, she'd gotten into the habit of neglecting her own pains. Besides, she hadn't wanted to worry her children.

"What is with this family?" Seth asked in exasperation on Saturday, the third day of LaDonna's hospitalization. He looked from one Baker sibling to the other as they rested for a few minutes in a visitors' lounge while their mother was undergoing another test. "Meagan ignored the signs of her ovarian torsion for so long she finally had to have emergency surgery. Now LaDonna has suffered in silence until she collapsed. You may be a family of doctors and caretakers, but all of you have to start taking care of yourselves, too."

"Amen," Jacqui said, entering the waiting room with a tote bag full of cold drinks and snacks.

"You're one to talk," Mitch accused her, even as he gratefully accepted a diet soda. Having just spent the past eight hours straight working before breaking away to check on his mother, he needed the caffeine. "Who's been taking care of all of us for the past few days?"

Jacqui's gaze met his for a few moments, but then she looked quickly away, moving to hand a drink to Madison. She had been attentive to Mitch during this crisis but in no different a way than with any of the others. He suspected that he was the only one who could detect the invisible wall she'd placed between them, holding him at a distance even as she had seen to his needs.

There had been more than one time during the past three days when Mitch would have liked to just take her into his arms and hold her, seeking courage and reassurance from her when his own had wavered at the thought of losing his mom. Had it not been for that imaginary wall, and for knowing how important it was to her not to let his family know about their brief affair, he might well have given in to the impulse.

"I've been making sure I've had plenty of rest and food during the past couple of days," Jacqui commented. "You guys are the ones who have to be reminded."

"Whatever you pay her, Seth, it isn't enough," Madison remarked, popping the top on her soda can. "Thank you, Jacqui. I needed this."

Mitch wondered if he was the only one who saw the slight wince narrow Jacqui's eyes for a moment before she moved on to hand Alice a bottle of flavored water. He knew very well that Jacqui hadn't been looking after them because she was paid to do so but because she genuinely cared about this family. She loved Alice and Seth and Meagan. She loved LaDonna.

Being loved by Jacqui Handy was a very special gift. Loving her in return was impossible to resist—at least for him, he realized abruptly.

He sank heavily into a straight-backed visitors' chair, nearly splashing soda on the white coat he wore over his blue surgical scrubs. As if he hadn't had enough shocks in the past few days, now he had a new one to deal with. He was in love with Jacqui. He'd been an idiot not to admit it earlier, especially when he'd been fortunate enough to be with her. Not to mention during the long, lonely nights that had passed after she'd sent him away.

With typical Baker oblivion, he had completely missed the symptoms of his own condition. He'd even misdiagnosed the signs that should have been glaringly obvious. Had he waited too long to do anything about it? Or had he ever really had a chance with Jacqui in the first place?

He watched her chatting with Seth across the room, both of them smiling. Probably lamenting together on how dense the Baker clan could be when it came to their own well-being. Now that it was apparent that LaDonna would make a complete recovery, everyone had relaxed a little, although he suspected his sisters were still struggling with the same guilt he was that they hadn't been more observant.

He wished he knew how to approach Jacqui with his new realization. Should he ask her out again, try to start all over with her? Or simply tell her the truth—that he missed her, that he'd been a fool to take so long to figure out what he'd been looking for all this time?

Would she give him another chance, or would she build yet another invisible wall between them? When would the time be right—if ever—for him to tell her what he felt?

Jacqui jabbed the doorbell button at LaDonna's house Sunday morning before she could change her mind. Mitch had moved out of the hotel and into his mother's house since she'd been hospitalized. Jacqui had driven there straight from an early visit with LaDonna. She had taken fresh flowers to decorate the hospital room in preparation for the after-church visitors who were sure to stop by later that day, and after talking with LaDonna, she had immediately come in search of Mitch.

She had taken a risk that he'd still be here. His car was in the driveway, so it looked as though she'd arrived in time to catch him. She was a little nervous but determined to talk to him.

He looked surprised when he opened the door to him. He smiled automatically to greet her, then stopped smiling in response to her expression. "What's wrong? Has something else happened?"

"Why did you cancel your trip to Peru?" she demanded without preamble.

He frowned. "What?"

"I just left your mom's room. She's very upset with you for canceling your trip."

"How did she find out? I haven't even told her yet."

"One of your friends told Madison, who told your mother, who told me. Why, Mitch?"

"Come inside, okay? No need to have this conversation on the porch." He ushered her in and closed the door behind her before saying, "I would think it's obvious why I canceled. I can't take a trip to South America with my mother just out of the hospital."

"She knew that was the reason, and she feels terrible about it. Your trip isn't for another two weeks. She'll be out of the hospital long before that, and your sisters and I will be here to take care of her. There's no need for you to stay."

"I just want to make sure she's okay. It'll take a couple of weeks for her to get her strength back and for us to make sure the treatments are working well and that she hasn't done any lasting damage. Anemia can wreak havoc on internal organs, even weaken the heart, you know."

"Your mother's heart has been checked very carefully, and it's undamaged," Jacqui shot back. "She'll have a period of recuperation, but I've heard the doctors say they expect a complete recovery. With proper treatment and precautions, she'll be just fine."

"Still, I'll be around to keep an eye on her here. I know you and Meagan and Maddie will all be available to her, but I need to know for myself that she's okay."

Jacqui planted her hands on her hips and studied his face with a frown. She read him very well these days. "You're blaming yourself because she got so sick, aren't you?"

Pushing a hand through his hair, he sighed. "You tried to tell me. I should have listened."

"She kept telling you she was fine, Mitch. You couldn't read her mind."

"No, but I should have seen just how thin and pale she had become. I was too wrapped up in my own issues, with work and the fire and planning for the trip and…"

And with her, she added mentally when his voice trailed off.

"Go on your trip, Mitch," she said more gently. "You've been looking forward to it for so long. Your mother wants you to go. She'll feel awful if you miss it because of her."

"It's too late," he said with a slight shrug. "I've already canceled. I called first thing Thursday morning. I lost my deposit, but that's no big deal. I'd rather stay here and make sure Mom's okay. To be honest, I'd sort of lost enthusiasm about the trip anyway."

Frowning, she took a step closer to him, trying to determine if that was the truth. "But why? You were so excited about it."

"Because you weren't going to be there," he answered simply.

She stared at him in shock. That was one answer she had not expected at all. "I don't—"

"I didn't want to go that far away from you. Not until I had a chance to tell you how much I've missed seeing you. Being with you. I've been trying to find the right time, the right words, to convince you that we're a perfect match, no matter how different our backgrounds might be."

"I, uh— I think I need to sit down." She sank onto

LaDonna's comfortable, overstuffed flowered couch, her head spinning a little.

Mitch sat beside her, looking at her so intently she flushed. "I'm not sure what you're trying to say," she admitted, having been completely unprepared for this conversation.

"I'm trying to say I love you, Jacqui. Something I should have told you the night you sent me away."

Shock jolted through her again, making her glad she was sitting down this time. "You...?"

"You said I wasn't ready for a permanent commitment, that I was afraid to sign a long-term lease—and maybe for a little while I wondered if you were right. Mostly I wondered if you weren't just using that for an excuse because you weren't interested in the long run with me."

"You're the one who said you wanted to keep your options open," she pointed out, her voice not quite steady.

"Yes, I did say that. I was looking for something, and for a time, I figured I needed to go somewhere else to find it. I guess I thought that because I hadn't been able to leave Little Rock, that must mean what I was searching for lay out there somewhere. But the truth is, I've been free to leave for months. My residency was almost finished, my mother and sisters were well and I didn't have a lease. Yet I stopped sending out applications to other hospitals about a year ago. Just about the time I met you. I was just too dense to make the connection until now."

She remembered him telling her how clearly he remembered that first meeting. That he had been attracted to her then and had wanted ever since to get to know her better. She'd been shocked then by that admission—she was even more stunned by what he was telling her now. *He loved her?*

"But you said you didn't even want to sign a lease," she said weakly. She knew she was repeating herself, but she couldn't seem to think clearly.

With an impatient shake of his head, he reached out to rest a hand on her shoulder. "You keep looking for hidden meanings in my lack of interest in real estate. I don't care whether I live in a house or an apartment or a condo or a tent, for that matter. I just hope there's a chance that someday you'll live there with me. I love you, Jacqui."

Her mind whirled with all the arguments she'd given herself. "I don't want to be another anchor around your neck. I don't want to be the reason you look back someday with regrets about the things you never got to do."

"I can still do anything I want. I can travel on vacations—with you, I hope. Maybe you'll enjoy traveling again when you know you have a permanent home to return to when the trip is over."

That was exactly the way she'd felt about traveling lately. Knowing she wouldn't have to keep pulling up roots and trying to settle somewhere new made it somewhat more tempting to see different places just for pleasure.

Before she could respond, Mitch added, "I don't see my family as anchors, Jacqui. I love them very much, and I treasure the time we're able to spend together. I don't blame any of them for the circumstances that kept me here in the past—it was always ultimately my choice to remain close to them when I thought they needed me. Just as it is my choice to stay close to Mom now while she recuperates rather than traipse around Peru with some people I like but who don't mean anything to me in comparison to my family. Or to you."

She drew a deep breath. "I've been trying so hard not to fall for you."

That smile of his was impossible to resist. "How's that been working for you?"

She placed a hand on his cheek. "Not so well."

Catching her hand, he placed a kiss in her palm. "You? The incomparably efficient Jacqui Handy? You never fail at anything."

"Of course I do," she said with a low sigh.

He stopped smiling. "If you're talking about the wreck, that wasn't your failure."

"I know," she said quietly. "Which doesn't mean I won't always feel some measure of guilt about it."

He kissed her hand again, then lowered it to his lap, his fingers laced with hers. "Any time you want to talk about it, I'm here, okay? And any time you need a distraction, I'm here for that, too. Let's just say I'm here for the duration. Whatever you need from me."

Tears threatened, but she blinked them back. "I'm not used to that."

"You'll have plenty of time to get used to it," he promised. "The rest of our lives, if you'll have me that long."

This conversation was scaring the heck out of her, she thought candidly—but he certainly knew the right things to say to tempt her to take risks.

"There are other problems between us," she said—as much to herself as to him.

He sighed with exaggerated patience. "You don't want to be Cinderella. The doctor and the housekeeper thing. I can tell you right now, that's bogus. No one, least of all me, cares to judge what you choose to do with your time. You want to keep running my sister's household and trying to keep my teenage niece in line, I say go for it. You're good at it. But if there are other things you want to pursue, I'll back you in that, too. I know you can do whatever you set your mind to, Jacqui."

She looked down at their interlaced hands. "There are still things you don't know about me."

"I look forward to learning them all."

"I never finished high school," she blurted in a rush. "I dropped out when my parents moved the last time. I got an equivalency degree a few years later, but I don't have the education your family values so much."

"Nobody cares about the framed papers hanging on your wall," he said with a shrug. "If you want to take college classes in something that interests you, do it. I can't imagine you having any difficulty with any subject. If more school doesn't interest you, don't do it. Believe it or not, I don't choose my friends by the degrees they hold. For that matter, I've played soccer every Sunday for years with a few people I consider friends, and I couldn't tell you for certain if they went to college or dropped out of school in junior high."

"You have an answer for everything, don't you?"

He smiled crookedly. "Not really. I'm still waiting for you to tell me how you feel about me."

She swallowed hard. "I… I think I love you, too," she whispered.

His face lit up again with his beautiful smile. "I'll take that—for now."

There were so many things still to be settled between them, she thought. How would his family react to him getting involved with her? How would she fit in with his friends? And she still didn't know what would happen between her and his family if for some reason she and Mitch couldn't make this work. But that no longer seemed to matter quite so much. As much as she cared for the rest of his family, her feelings for Mitch were stronger. If she had to make the hard choice between him and them at this moment—she would have to choose Mitch.

The realization actually surprised her with its sudden clarity.

"But," she warned quickly, fending him off when he would have tugged her toward him, "I'm not committing to anything just yet. We need to take our time. We need to be sure any decisions we make are what we both want, what's best for both of us. We shouldn't…"

"We shouldn't sign any long-term leases just yet?"

His teasing interruption made her flush a little, even though she had to smile. "You're the one who said we should stop with the real-estate metaphors."

"They do seem to keep cropping up, don't they?"

She reached up to grab his collar and tug lightly. "Maybe we should just stop talking for now."

He smiled against her lips. "I've been waiting for you to say that."

She wrapped her arms around his neck and snuggled into his embrace, deciding they could deal with any potential issues later. They had more pressing matters to attend to just now.

They lay snuggled together in the bed in Mitch's old bedroom, though he commented that the decor had changed a bit since he'd lived there last. The sports and rock-band posters had been replaced by earth-toned paint and landscape prints. LaDonna had kept a masculine feel to the room so Mitch would be comfortable whenever he stayed there. Jacqui tried not to think about LaDonna's reaction to what had just taken place in this room.

Such speculation didn't seem to be disturbing Mitch. He looked quite pleased with himself, actually, as he smiled at her from the pillow beside hers. "I'm very glad you stopped by today," he said. "I've been wondering how to get you alone to talk about my feelings for you. I didn't expect you to show up on the doorstep today."

"I was so perturbed when your mother told me about you canceling your trip to Peru that I guess I just stormed over here without giving myself a chance to think about it," she admitted.

"Because you didn't want me to be disappointed about missing the trip. I'm touched by that, Jacqui."

"Maybe I just wanted to get you out of the country for a few days."

He chuckled. "Sorry to disappoint you."

"You're sure you don't want to—"

"I'm sure," he cut in. "So, how would you like to maybe go to Peru with me this time next year?"

Her smile wavered a bit, though she kept her tone light. "That's very long-term planning."

"True. But that's one deposit I wouldn't hesitate to make. I keep telling you, I'm in this for the long-term, Jacqui."

The more he said it, the more believable it sounded. And although she was still afraid to let herself believe too much in what she wanted so badly, she had to trust that he meant what he said.

He let out a long breath. "Guess I should get dressed and head over to the hospital to see Mom. I need to reassure her that missing the trip to Peru isn't the worst thing that's ever happened to me. Want to go with me?"

The question was seemingly casual, but she knew

exactly what it meant. If she and Mitch went together to the hospital now, there would be no more pretending that they were merely friends. "All right."

His smile curved his nice mouth and gleamed in his blue eyes. "Thank you."

Drawing a deep breath, she told herself she would take almost any risk in exchange for Mitch's beautiful smile. "I'm a little nervous," she admitted.

"I know. But I'll be right there beside you. Now and for always. I love you, Jacqui."

She leaned over to kiss his smile. "I love you, too."

How could she not? She'd been searching for Mitch all her life.

Epilogue

Six days later, Jacqui stood beside Mitch on the sidewalk outside the house in Hillcrest, gazing at the front door with a bone-deep longing. The keys to that door dangled in Mitch's hand, and she wanted nothing more than for him to open it and let her walk inside to explore again. He'd borrowed the keys from the Realtor who'd shown them the house before, saying he wanted to look at the place with Jacqui one more time before making an offer—just to make sure this was the right choice.

It was still hot on this first Saturday in September. The sky was a deep, cloudless blue overhead, the afternoon sun beating down on the heat-shriveled trees and grass. A few flowers still bloomed in the beds, but their colors were fading and the beds needed tending. Jacqui's fingers itched to play in those small gardens, weeding and pruning and planting colorful mums for the coming fall. She would rest between chores with a glass of lemonade on that lovely porch, she thought wistfully, her gaze moving to the inviting wood rockers. This was exactly the house she had always dreamed of.

She turned resolutely away. "I don't think you should buy it," she said abruptly to Mitch.

He looked at her in visible surprise. "I thought you loved this house."

"I do," she had to admit, because she was always honest with him. "It's perfect. But you shouldn't buy it for that reason."

He spun to face her fully. "Jacqui, you know I'm hoping you'll share this house with me. I've gotten accustomed to having you under the same roof. Even more accustomed to sharing a bed," he added in a low, affectionately teasing tone that brought warmth to her cheeks.

"And I will live with you," she assured him around a lump in her throat. "But I want you to make very sure it's what *you* want before you commit to a purchase this big."

She drew a deep breath. "If you still want to try living in a few other places before you buy a house and settle in for the long-term, I think you should do it, Mitch. As for me—I'll go where you go. I'll support you completely in whatever you need to do, just as you've promised to do for me."

For the first time in her life, she understood her mother a little better. Troubled as she was in so many ways, Cindy Handy loved her husband and she wanted to be with him wherever he drifted. Jacqui was dissimilar from her mother, and she had different priorities in her life—for one thing, if she ever had children, which she hoped to do someday, she would strive to give them much more of a sense of security and emotional support than she and Olivia had received. But she understood now what her mother had meant when she'd said that "home" wasn't necessarily a place but a feeling.

As much as she loved living in Little Rock, Jacqui understood now that she could make a home with Mitch wherever they went. For one thing, she knew he would always put her needs and desires first—something her own rather selfish father had been unable to do for anyone else. The fact that Mitch was willing to buy this house just because he knew she loved it, that he had always put his loved ones' best interests ahead of his own, was all the proof she needed that she had given her heart and her trust to the right man.

Mitch took both her hands in his, the keys cupped between his right palm and her left. His eyes were dark with emotion when he gazed down at her, his mouth curved in a loving smile. "The fact that you offered to move away with me means more than you could ever possibly realize. I know exactly how hard it must have been for you to make that offer. You love it here."

"I love you more," she said, her voice a bit shaky now.

He leaned down to brush a kiss over her lips, oblivious to the car passing on the street behind them, to anyone in neighboring yards who might see them. Again unlike her parents, Mitch was open with his emotions, unabashed at having anyone see that he was in love with her.

He had made it clear to his family that he had chosen Jacqui for his life partner. It wasn't as if this was a decision they'd made overnight, he had added when they had reacted with delighted surprise. He'd been in love with Jacqui for more than a year. He'd just been a little slow to do anything about it, he'd admitted.

Jacqui had been overwhelmed with gratitude by how enthusiastically Mitch's family had approved his choice. Especially his mother, who was recovering nicely from her health scare under the watchful eyes of her still-guilt-ridden physician children. LaDonna confided that she'd watched Mitch's behavior around Jacqui for several months with a suspicion that he was smitten, and she couldn't have been more delighted to have been proved right.

As for Alice, she smugly claimed credit, saying she really should go into the matchmaking business some-day rather than orthodontia. She also claimed respon-sibility for getting her dad and Meagan together.

"I am exactly where I want to be," Mitch assured Jacqui now. "My family is here, my work is here, but most importantly, you are here. I can't imagine any other place on this planet having more to offer me."

After twenty-nine years of protecting herself from disappointment, it was difficult to put so much faith in anyone else. But she was getting there with Mitch. "Just don't rush into it on my behalf," she said. "There will always be other houses if you want to keep looking for a while."

He nodded, squeezing her hands before dropping his own. She noted that he had passed the keys to her. She wrapped her fingers around them, feeling the tug of temptation to use them.

"I was thinking that porch could be taken down and replaced with a sunroom," Mitch commented, turning to eye the front of the house again. "Maybe brick with lots of glass. And all that stained wood inside? Maybe we could update it a little. You know, paint it white or something."

She gasped. "You will do no such thing! That porch

is perfect. And don't you even think about getting near that beautiful wood trim with a paintbrush. This house is—"

She fell silent when she saw the grin cross his face.

"Yours," he finished for her in somewhat smug satisfaction. "This house is yours. It has been from the first moment you saw it. Might as well admit it."

Her knees went weak as her fingers tightened spasmodically around the keys to her dream house. "Fine," she managed to say after a moment. "But I'm putting my savings toward the down payment."

"That isn't necessary. I—"

She poked his shoulder with one finger as they moved toward the front door. "I haven't worked and saved for the past ten years just to have someone come along and buy a house for me, Mitchell Baker. I told you, I'm no Cinderella. Maybe this is a nicer house than I could have afforded on my own—okay, it's definitely more than I could have managed—but that doesn't mean I won't be fully invested in owning it. It won't be all mine—or all yours. It will be ours."

"Ours," he repeated. "I like the sound of that."

"So do I," she said, her vision misty as she fitted the key into the lock of the house they would make into a home together. "So do I."

* * * * *

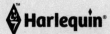
Harlequin®

COMING NEXT MONTH

Available June 28, 2011

SPECIAL EDITION

USA TODAY *bestselling author B.J. Daniels*
takes you on a trip to Whitehorse, Montana,
and the Chisholm Cattle Company.

RUSTLED

Available July 2011 from Harlequin Intrigue.

As the dust settled, Dawson got his first good look at the rustler. A pair of big Montana sky-blue eyes glared up at him from a face framed by blond curls.

A woman rustler?

"You have to let me go," she hollered as the roar of the stampeding cattle died off in the distance.

"So you can finish stealing my cattle? I don't think so." Dawson jerked the woman to her feet.

She reached for the gun strapped to her hip hidden under her long barn jacket.

He grabbed the weapon before she could, his eyes narrowing as he assessed her. "How many others are there?" he demanded, grabbing a fistful of her jacket. "I think you'd better start talking before I tear into you."

She tried to fight him off, but he was on to her tricks and pinned her to the ground. He was suddenly aware of the soft curves beneath the jean jacket she wore under her coat.

"You have to listen to me." She ground out the words from between her gritted teeth. "You have to let me go. If you don't they will come back for me and they will kill you. There are too many of them for you to fight off alone. You won't stand a chance and I don't want your blood on my hands."

"I'm touched by your concern for me. Especially after you just tried to pull a gun on me."

"I wasn't going to shoot you."

Dawson hauled her to her feet and walked her the rest of the way to his horse. Reaching into his saddlebag, he pulled out a length of rope.

"You can't tie me up."

He pulled her hands behind her back and began to tie her wrists together.

"If you let me go, I can keep them from coming back," she said. "You have my word." She let out an unladylike curse. "I'm just trying to save your sorry neck."

"And I'm just going after my cattle."

"Don't you mean your boss's cattle?"

"Those cattle are mine."

"*You're* a Chisholm?"

"Dawson Chisholm. And you are…?"

"Everyone calls me Jinx."

He chuckled. "I can see why."

Bronco busting, falling in love…it's all in a day's work.
Look for the rest of their story in

RUSTLED

Available July 2011 from Harlequin Intrigue
wherever books are sold.

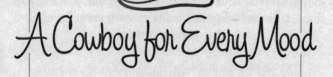

SPECIAL EDITION

Life, Love and Family

THE TEXANS ARE COMING!

Reader-favorite miniseries Montana Mavericks is back in Special Edition with new loves, adventures and more.

July 2011 features *USA TODAY* bestselling author

CHRISTINE RIMMER

with

RESISTING MR. TALL, DARK & TEXAN.

A Texas oil mogul arrives in Thunder Canyon on business and soon falls for his personal assistant. Only one problem—she's just resigned to open a bakery! Can he convince her to stay on—as his bride?

Find out in July!

Look for a new
Montana Mavericks: The Texans Are Coming title
in each of these months

August	September	October
November	December	

Available wherever books are sold.

www.Harlequin.com